D0776706

BAYSIDE
MaDNESS

"Saved by the Bell" titles include:

Mark-Paul Gosselaar: Ultimate Gold

Mario Lopez: High-Voltage Star

Behind the Scenes at "Saved by the Bell"

Beauty and Fitness with "Saved by the Bell"

▲ ▼ ▲

Hot new fiction titles:

Zack Strikes Back

Bayside Madness

California Scheming

Girls' Night Out

Zack's Last Scam

Class Trip Chaos

BAYSIDE MaDNESS

by Beth Cruise

Collier Books
Macmillan Publishing Company
New York

Maxwell Macmillan Canada
Toronto

Maxwell Macmillan International
New York   Oxford   Singapore   Sydney

Collier Books   Maxwell Macmillan Canada, Inc.
Macmillan Publishing Company   1200 Eglinton Avenue East
866 Third Avenue   Suite 200
New York, NY 10022   Don Mills, Ontario M3C 3N1

Macmillan Publishing Company is part of the Maxwell Communication
Group of Companies.

First Collier Books edition 1992
Printed in the United States of America
10   9   8   7   6   5   4   3

Library of Congress Cataloging-in-Publication Data

Cruise, Beth.
Bayside Madness / by Beth Cruise.
p. cm.
Summary: When Bayside High's Wacky Wednesday backfires, Zack Morris
and the "Saved by the Bell" gang try to get things back to normal.
ISBN 0-02-042775-1
[1. High schools—Fiction.   2. Schools—Fiction.]   I. Title.
PZ7.C88827Zac   1992
[Fic]—dc20
91-46070

BAYSIDE
MADNESS

To the
"Saved by the Bell" cast

Chapter 1

Nobody at Bayside High could believe it. The lottery *must* have been fixed. Or Zack Morris had come up with another one of his schemes and rigged the results. How else could the biggest troublemaker at school have gotten picked to replace the principal on Student-Teacher Role-Reversal Day?

Zack Morris heard the grumbling, but he ignored it as easily as a *C* minus on a history quiz. He smiled at himself in the bathroom mirror of the Max, the Bayside High hangout. He smoothed back his blond hair and practiced his killer grin.

"Definitely principal material," he told his reflection. If he were the principal, Mr. Belding—and he *would* be Mr. Belding, starting at 9:00 A.M. tomorrow—he would be mighty nervous about this role-reversal business. Zack had all the qualities a leader needed most—terrific looks, charisma, and good dental work. Not to mention an ability to stretch the truth under the most dire circumstances.

Zack sighed and straightened his collar. He wouldn't be surprised if the entire student body voted to keep him on as principal for good!

No one had been more surprised than Zack when his name had been announced as Mr. Belding's replacement. For once, he *hadn't* schemed or bent the rules to win. He was the winner, fair and square, to take over for Mr. Belding on Wacky Wednesday, which was Mr. Belding's corny term for the experiment tomorrow. Mr. Belding actually saw Wacky Wednesday as a chance for students to see how difficult the teachers' jobs were. He thought it would foster mutual understanding and respect. Everyone else at Bayside High saw it as a chance to get out of doing homework.

Zack left the men's room and entered the Max. Students were ordering milk shakes, eating hamburgers, and talking a mile a minute about Wacky Wednesday, which was now—Zack checked his watch—a mere seventeen hours away. *Seventeen hours to glory*, Zack thought with a happy sigh. Bayside High would never be the same.

Zack spread his arms. "It's your leader," he announced. Everyone booed.

"Who wants detention tomorrow?" Zack asked

mischievously and the boos immediately changed to cheers. Zack acknowledged them with a wave and started toward his table.

"Oh, Zack?" Daisy Tyler stood up and touched his arm. She was a terrific-looking cheerleader with curly blond hair and light blue eyes. "I have the teensiest little problem," she cooed. "Terrible Testaverde is totally on my case about my social studies grade. Do you think you could have a talk with him?"

Zack hesitated. There was nothing he would have liked better at that moment than to drown in Daisy Tyler's baby blue eyes and promise her the moon. But lately he'd begun to realize that there was only one particular pair of blue eyes he truly wanted to drown in. They were deep blue, they sparkled, and they belonged to the head cheerleader, Kelly Kapowski.

Zack had known Kelly all his life. He'd probably fallen in love with her when she'd dumped a pail of sand on his head in the sandbox. They'd been in and out of love ever since, and junior year they'd even gone steady. They'd broken up near the end of the school year, and at the time they'd both thought it was the best thing. They needed to experiment with other people, they'd told each other solemnly. *I must have been nuts!* Zack thought.

It had taken him a while, but he'd finally realized

what he should have known all along—Kelly was the only girl for him. Now all he had to do was get Kelly to realize it.

He patted Daisy's hand, then returned it to her side. "I'll think about it, Daisy," he said.

"Zack, can you get me out of English tomorrow?" someone called.

Zack waved a careless hand. "Line up for requests tomorrow morning, folks."

He continued toward his table, where he saw his friends already gathered. Kelly was the only one missing: She'd probably gotten tied up at school. Jessie, Lisa, and Slater were acting pretty unimpressed with the principal-to-be, but Zack knew it was just a front.

"Don't get up, guys," he advised everyone loftily.

"Don't worry about it, preppie," A. C. Slater said. His deep brown eyes twinkled. "We weren't even thinking about it." He took another bite of his deluxe cheeseburger.

"If you keep eating those cheeseburgers, Slater, you'll have to be lifted onto the mat with a crane at your next meet," Zack observed. Slater was the captain of the wrestling and football teams. He was a little too successful with girls, in Zack's opinion. It always blew Zack away when girls chose brawn like Slater's over brains like his.

Slater lifted one arm. "See this, Morris? It's a

muscle. You probably have a hard time recognizing it." He laughed and shook his dark curly head. Slater liked his own jokes better than anybody else's.

Zack rolled his eyes and slid in the booth next to Lisa Turtle. She was a gorgeous, petite black teen who was crazy about clothes and boys—and she had a hard time deciding in which order.

"I'm glad you're here, Zack," Jessie Spano said crisply from across the table. "I have some ideas for tomorrow." Jessie was a pretty girl with a first-rate mind and legs that went on forever. But she was less concerned with being a knockout than she was about saving the world.

She tossed her long, curly brown ponytail behind her shoulder and reached into her backpack to pull out a stack of pages. "First of all, I think a consciousness-raising class for girls is a must."

Slater smirked. "Never mind consciousness-raising, Jessie. I'd like to see some *hemline* raising."

"Miniskirts—all *right*!" Zack chimed in. He reached out to high-five Slater. Their friendship may have had a competitive edge, but guys had to stick together where miniskirts were involved.

"Sorry to have to tell you this, boys," Lisa said, her dark brown eyes concerned. "But I hear that hemlines are going down this fall." She sighed tragically. "I still haven't gotten over it."

"Cut it out, you guys," Jessie complained. "I'm

serious. Zack can really make a difference, even if it is only for a day."

"That's exactly what I was thinking," Slater put in. "I have an idea, too."

"You do?" Jessie asked, surprised. "Congratulations. This must be a first. I mean, usually ideas are the result of a thinking process."

The rest of the kids rolled their eyes. They were used to Jessie and Slater's sparring. Everyone knew that deep down, Jessie and Slater were crazy about each other, even though they would never admit it. Opposites definitely attracted in this case, but Jessie and Slater couldn't make it through a Saturday-night date without an argument.

Jessie and Slater's last date had been at Lisa's pool party. During an argument, Jessie had thrown Slater into the pool. He'd sworn he'd never go out with her again, and Jessie had seconded the motion. Zack had led the betting on who would break down first. The odds were ten to one that Slater would cave in.

Slater cleared his throat and threw Jessie a dirty look. "As I was saying," he went on, turning to Zack, "I have an idea. I think you should devote the whole afternoon to P.E. tomorrow. I'd be glad to volunteer to teach the class."

"Well, there you go," Jessie said sadly. "I knew you'd get into trouble if you tried to use your brain. It's short-circuited completely."

"Is that smoke coming out of your ears, Slater?" Lisa giggled.

Slater ignored them. "I think P.E. is a crucial part of educating our young people," he said virtuously.

"On second thought, I can see you teaching P.E.," Jessie said thoughtfully. "Puerile education. It's a perfect match!"

Slater scowled at Jessie. He had no idea what *puerile* meant, but he knew an insult when he heard one.

"Chill out, you guys," Lisa said. She turned to Zack. "Here's my idea. A course called mall 101. It can't miss. You know how confusing it can be to hit the mall on a Saturday. I have it all timed—where to park, what entrance to use, what stores get crowded at what times, how to snag a dressing room . . ."

"Lisa, I think there are more important things students could learn about," Jessie said with a sigh.

Lisa looked puzzled. "There are?"

"Sounds great, Lisa," Zack said. "But I think Mr. Belding would freak, don't you?"

"Are you kidding?" Lisa sniffed as she smoothed her flowered denim skirt. "Have you noticed his wardrobe lately? He should be the first to sign up."

Just then, Samuel Powers, better known as Screech, ran into the Max. Screech was a skinny bundle of excited nerves, with a spectacularly illogical mind and an amazingly elastic face. He was wearing a pair of striped pants with a pink shirt and purple suspenders. He skidded to a stop in front of Zack, his frizzy curls bouncing wildly.

"Zack, I have an idea," he said.

"Not another one!" Jessie groaned, and everyone laughed.

"Don't worry," Lisa confided. "If it's coming from Screech, we don't have to pay attention."

Screech shot her an adoring look. He never minded when Lisa teased him. He worshiped her, and any kind of attention was better than nothing.

"It's about tomorrow," he told Zack.

Zack sighed. Not another request! This principal business was harder than he'd thought. He couldn't even drink his soda in peace.

"I think you should make a stand for animal rights," Screech declared.

Jessie nodded vigorously. "That's a great idea, Screech. Whales or dolphins?"

"Mice!" Screech exclaimed. "Zack, you can strike a blow for the rodent population that they'll never forget. Release all the mice in the science lab."

Lisa made a face. "Ewwww," she said. "No way!"

"But I already built them a corral out of ice-cream sticks," Screech protested. "They'll be totally comfortable."

"It's not *them* I'm worried about," Lisa told him.

Zack decided it was time to change the subject. "Where's Kelly?" he asked. "She should have been here fifteen minutes ago."

Jessic shrugged. "She was called to Mr. Belding's office after the last bell."

Zack shook his head sadly. "Poor Kelly. Sent to the principal's office two days in a row."

"What do you mean?" Jessie asked. "Kelly wasn't in the principal's office on Monday."

"I'm talking about tomorrow," Zack said with a sly grin. "I have the feeling she's going to need a private conference."

"Zack, I thought you and Kelly were through," Lisa said, puzzled. "You guys decided to be just friends."

Whoops. Zack wanted Kelly to be the first person to find out that he wanted them back on track. Their new romance just had to start out right. They were seniors now. They would have a mature, sophisticated relationship. No more schemes. No more fibs. Total honesty. Total commitment. A whole new Zack.

"Kelly and I *are* through, Lisa," he lied sincerely. "I was just kidding."

Just then, Kelly burst into the Max. Her skin was glowing, her blue eyes were sparkling, and her long, shiny dark hair was flying. Her tanned and shapely legs looked great in a short mini. Zack watched her as she crossed the Max toward their table. Her lush smile seemed aimed at him.

That's my girl, he thought proudly, smiling back. Their gazes intertwined, and he felt an electric current pass between them. Kelly was still crazy about him, he just knew it. It wouldn't be hard at all to win her back. She was probably just waiting for him to suggest it. Girls were shy that way.

"Hi, guys," Kelly said breathlessly as she slid into the booth across from Zack.

"Hi, Kelly," Zack said. He could tell his hello meant something special to her. He gave her that trademark charismatic beam from his hazel eyes. She melted a little, he was sure of it.

"What took so long with Mr. Belding?" Jessie asked curiously. "Are you in trouble?"

Kelly smiled as she shook her head. "Not at all," she said. "He—"

"Kelly, can I order something for you?" Zack asked her. He gave her a soulful look.

"Oh, thanks, Zack," Kelly said warmly. "I'm dying for a diet root beer."

She'd ordered a soda, but Zack knew what she'd really meant. By the look in her eyes, he knew she was saying *I'm dying for you, Zack.*

Kelly leaned forward. Zack looked into her deep blue eyes. He wished everyone would go away so that he could be alone with her. Then they could get the reconciliation over with and concentrate on the important things—like going to a drive-in.

"Anyway," Kelly said to the gang, "I have such great news. Mr. Belding called me in to tell me about this new transfer student. He asked me if I'd watch out for him, show him around and all that stuff. He even enrolled him in my classes."

"Why is he asking you to baby-sit?" Jessie asked.

"Is he cute?" Lisa interrupted.

Kelly closed her eyes. "Cute doesn't begin to describe him."

Zack laughed. "That bad, huh?"

"He's *gorgeous*," Kelly squealed.

Zack got a sinking feeling in his stomach. But maybe he was just hungry. After all, even if the guy was gorgeous, that didn't mean Kelly would really go for him. She wasn't a shallow person. The guy was probably a conceited jerk. Once she got to know him, she wouldn't give him the time of day.

"And the reason that Mr. Belding asked me to help out is because I already know him," Kelly continued. "He's Cody Durant!"

Zack wasn't sinking anymore—he was drowning. And the name Cody Durant might as well have been his death toll. He knew the name, even though he'd never met the guy. Kelly had met Cody the summer before last. He'd been staying at his father's house on the beach, and Kelly had fallen for him at first sight. They'd been inseparable for the whole month of August. Luckily, Zack had been on vacation with his family at the time, so he hadn't had to watch Kelly fall in love with someone else.

But now he'd have to watch it, and he didn't like it one bit. Kelly's sparkling eyes, her smile, her breathless voice were all because of *Cody Durant*?

"You mean that guy you fell for last summer?" Jessie asked. "The one from San Francisco?"

Kelly nodded. "I can't wait to see him again."

"He's gorgeous," Lisa breathed. "You're so lucky."

Kelly sighed happily. "I know."

"Settle down, girls," Slater said uneasily. "I mean, how gorgeous can the guy be?"

Jessie, Lisa, and Kelly turned to him. *"Gorgeous,"* they all said together.

Screech nodded vigorously. "He is, Slater. I met him. His body is even better than mine."

Lisa gave Screech a pitying look. "A flagpole has a better body than you do."

"Thanks, Lisa," Screech said sincerely. "I've been working out lately. I was hoping you'd notice."

Zack hardly heard them. His day had slid downhill, and fast. Ten minutes ago, he'd been on top of the world. But now he had to face the fact that some other guy had captured his girl. Because Kelly *was* his girl—no matter who else she happened to date. Zack knew that for sure. But how could he get Kelly to realize it?

Weakly, Zack signaled the waiter for Kelly's root beer. He wondered if he'd finally met his match. Cody Durant was the only other guy Kelly had gone absolutely wild about. How could Zack compete against that?

James, the waiter, approached with his pad. "So what'll it be, *Principal* Morris?" Obviously, he'd heard the gossip in the Max.

That was it! Zack broke out in a dazzling smile. Why hadn't he thought of it before? Maybe *Zack* would be powerless to separate Kelly from Cody Durant. But Principal Morris had power. He would be like a dictator, and Bayside High would be his country. Taking care of one little hunk of a surfer would be a breeze!

Chapter 2

On Wednesday, Zack actually made it to school on time. It was a truly rare occasion. He hurried underneath the Wacky Wednesday banner the Art Club had made, on his way to Mr. Belding's office. He was completely ready to assume the great responsibility of ruling Bayside High. He wondered if he should ask the students to bow as they passed him. But maybe that was a little extreme.

Today he had decided that it was important to dress for the part, so he'd worn a tie with his jeans. Smoothing his hair and assuming a principallike expression, he knocked on Mr. Belding's door. He heard a muffled voice tell him to come in.

Zack opened the door and burst out laughing. Mr. Belding was wearing flowered Jams, high tops, and a neon orange baseball cap turned backward.

A message on his T-shirt read LIFE'S A BEACH.

Mr. Belding looked sheepish as Zack doubled up in hysterics. "All right, Zack," he said nervously. "Maybe I went a little overboard. I thought I should get into the spirit of things."

Zack forced his face into a serious expression. He nodded. "And you have, sir."

"Right. Well, let's get down to business," Mr. Belding said, crossing over to his desk. Zack cleared his throat loudly, and Mr. Belding stopped before sitting down.

Zack pointed at the chair. "Mine," he said.

Mr. Belding smiled meekly. "You're quite right, Zack."

"Mr. Morris," Zack said.

"Uh, right."

Zack smiled patiently and went around the desk. He gave Mr. Belding a gentle push and then sat in the principal's chair. He clasped his hands on the desk and gave Mr. Belding a severe look. "Now. Can I help you, young man?"

Mr. Belding frowned as he took the seat Zack usually occupied in front of the desk.

"Very funny, *Mister* Morris," he said. "Now, let's go over some rules about today, shall we? You can't overstep your bounds. This is a learning experience, not an opportunity to run wild. You understand me?"

"Absolutely, Mr. Belding," Zack assured him.

He wondered if Kelly and Cody had driven to
school together that morning. Maybe he should
have called Kelly last night and offered her a ride.

"Now, your job is to take care of whatever disci-
plinary problems crop up during the day. And you'll
also need to handle administrative tasks," Mr.
Belding continued. "But under no circumstances
can you alter any school policy or initiate any new
school activity." Mr. Belding was looking Zack in
the eye.

"Gee," Zack said with a sigh. "Does that mean
I have to cancel the Cheerleaders' Mud-Wrestling
Match?"

Mr. Belding shot him an exasperated look.

"I guess so," Zack murmured.

"Zack," Mr. Belding said, irritated, "this is a
serious exercise. The students should get a glimpse
of how difficult the teachers' jobs really are. It's not
a game. Now, let me outline some problems that
might crop up for you. First of all . . ."

Zack tuned out as Mr. Belding began to babble
something about Mr. Monza, the head of the maintenance staff. Zack had stayed awake last night
wondering how he would deal with Cody Durant.
As soon as Mr. Belding left, he would begin to put
his plan in motion.

"The principal is the one who holds the school
together," Mr. Belding continued. "The job isn't
easy, but the rewards are great. As a matter of fact,

Zack," he confided, "I'm a candidate for Principal of the Year. It's a great honor, and I wouldn't have gotten it if I hadn't taken my job as seriously as I do. There's a delicate balance between freedom and discipline. I hope you learn that today."

"Right," Zack said. The first bell rang, and he raised an eyebrow at Mr. Belding. "Shouldn't you be getting to homeroom? You don't want to get detention now, do you? How would that look for the Principal of the Year?"

"Oh, my," Mr. Belding said. He grabbed his neon orange backpack and skidded out of the room.

Zack leaned back in his chair and surveyed his office. "Not bad," he said aloud. He leaned over and buzzed Mrs. Gibbs, Mr. Belding's secretary.

A moment later she ran in, clutching her pad and pencil. "Good morning, Mr. Morris," she said. She adjusted her glasses, smoothed her crimped gray hair, and gave him a wobbly smile. Mrs. Gibbs tried her best, but she was the most disorganized person in the world. Nobody could figure out how she got anything done at all, least of all Mr. Belding.

"Good morning, Mrs. Gibbs," Zack said. "First of all, I'd like you to call the AV department and have them bring in a TV and VCR."

Mrs. Gibbs looked startled, but she made a note on her pad. "Certainly, Mr. Morris."

"And I didn't have time to have breakfast this morning—you know how rushed the principal biz can be—so will you order me up some eggs and hash browns from the Max? Just put it on the Bayside High account."

"But there isn't a Bayside High account, Mr. Morris."

"Well, I think it's high time there was one, don't you?" Zack tapped a pencil against the desk. "Start one today."

"Certainly, Mr. Morris." Mrs. Gibbs scribbled frantically on her pad, then looked up for the next instruction.

"Ah, yes." Zack tapped the desk. "Over easy, please."

Mrs. Gibbs looked shocked. "I beg your pardon? I'm an old woman, Mr. Morris. I can't do flips or things like that."

"Not you, Mrs. Gibbs," Zack said patiently. "The eggs. And for the last item—"

"Yes, Mr. Morris?"

"Get me a copy of Cody Durant's schedule. He's the new transfer student. And that's all for now."

As soon as Mrs. Gibbs scurried out, Zack leaned back in his chair. He had this principal business down. Nothing to it at all. He might even do some work after breakfast.

▲   ▼   ▲

"Class, no talking!" Jessie rapped out.

Slater stood up and hammered on his desk. "Miss Spano said no talking!" he yelled. As soon as the noise level went down, he grinned. "What she wants is singing!" he announced. Then he led the class in a ringing rendition of the Bayside High school song.

Jessie slumped back in her seat in frustration. She had been tapped to take over Mrs. Simpson's first-period English class, and so far her performance had been a dud. She couldn't get control of things at all. And it was all Slater's fault.

Before class, he'd informed her angrily that he'd actually looked up puerile in the dictionary last night. Before she could express her surprise that he even *had* a dictionary, Slater had informed her that he was going to get even.

Puerile meant immature, and Slater sure was proving it, Jessie thought despairingly. She really couldn't stand the arrogant, macho jerk.

If only he weren't such a *cute* arrogant, macho jerk. But she could control her baser impulses, Jessie told herself firmly. Just because Slater was major adorable didn't mean she couldn't resist him.

She pounded on the desk until the class stopped singing. Mrs. Simpson sat in the last row, smiling vaguely. She was so hard of hearing that she had no idea how out of control the class was.

"Enough!" Jessie snapped at the class.

"You want dancing instead?" Slater offered innocently.

Jessie leaned over the desk. "Slater," she said distinctly, "you can stick it."

"Really, Miss Spano? Where?" Slater asked devilishly.

"In your ear!" Jessie roared.

Mrs. Simpson perked up. She waved a hand. "No, no, dear," she said to Jessie. "Shakespeare was last term. We're doing Wordsworth now."

Jessie smiled thinly. "Yes, Mrs. Simpson. Okay, class, open your books to page ninety-eight."

Slater thumbed through his textbook. "We have to read a poem about *daffodils*? No way." He slammed his book shut and crossed his powerful arms. "I'm on strike."

Jessie had had it. She stood up and put her hands on her hips. "Fine. You're on strike. Go have a sit-in at the principal's office."

Slater stared at Jessie for a minute before he realized that she was serious. He looked unnerved. He'd never expected Jessie to throw him out of class. He stood up and picked up his books. "I wasn't going to learn anything, anyway," he said haughtily over his shoulder as he headed toward the door. The door banged against the wall as he flung it open. Furious, he stalked out without a backward look.

Jessie strode to the doorway. "You *never* learn

anything!'' she shouted after Slater. Then she shut
the door with a crash.

▲   ▼   ▲

In study hall, Kelly shifted in her chair. Her bare
knee brushed against Cody's jeans, sending an electric charge through her. Confused, she moved her
leg away again, then wished she hadn't.

Ever since Kelly had seen Cody again, she'd
been a bundle of nerves. One look at his dimples
and his crooked grin was enough to plunge her back
a year in time to when she'd first fallen for him. Of
course, since then, she'd fallen for Zack. But she
and Zack had agreed to be friends, and whatever
romantic feelings they'd had were buried. Now she
was free to love again. And it wasn't as hard to fall
in love with someone else as she'd imagined it
would be. No, Kelly thought, as her gaze wandered
over Cody's incredible body in his faded blue jeans
and T-shirt. It wasn't hard at all.

She still thought about Zack, of course. There
was a part of her that would always be crazy about
that blond charmer. But it was over, she told herself. And it was time for something new.

Cody looked at her and smiled. He had the deepest green eyes she'd ever seen, as clear as the
Pacific on a sunny morning. His longish black hair

was thick and unruly, and his hands looked strong. She could remember how he kissed, too. Kelly blushed and looked down, remembering.

"It's so cool to see you again, Kelly," Cody whispered. "I still can't believe I'm actually here."

"I can't believe it, either," she answered honestly. Normally, they wouldn't really be able to talk in study hall. But Vivian Mahoney was in charge, and she had a major crush on Walt Petronius. So far, she'd barely looked at the class. She was totally engrossed in helping Walt with his chemistry homework.

"I didn't think it was possible," Cody said. "But you're even prettier than I remembered."

Kelly smiled shyly, feeling embarrassed. The look in Cody's green eyes was totally sincere. He really liked her! Kelly had been a little worried that he wouldn't care about her anymore. After all, he'd never written to her after that summer. She remembered those trips to the mailbox every day, hoping to hear from him. But the memory of that heartbreak was far away now. Cody was here, right next to her, and he was just as wonderful as he used to be.

As if he could read her thoughts, Cody frowned. "I know I didn't write to you, Kelly," he said. "It wasn't that I didn't think about you. Maybe I thought about you *too* much. It was so hard to leave you that I didn't want to make it worse. If we'd kept writing to each other, I just would have been miserable not to have you. Not to mention that I'm not at my best on paper. I must have written a million letters and torn them up. I guess I was a coward. But that's what happened."

Cody reached out and took her hand. He played with her fingers, lacing his strong ones through her more slender ones. "It's hard to have a long-distance romance," he said softly. "But now that I'm here, I realize how stupid I was a year ago. I shouldn't have been afraid of looking like a fool. I should have written."

Kelly squeezed his fingers. "It's okay, Cody. You were probably right. Maybe it wasn't the right time for us."

Cody smiled. "Maybe now is," he said.

▲   ▼   ▲

In the principal's office, Zack bent over the memo he was writing. Slater was sitting on the couch, watching "The Young and the Reckless" on TV. He was finishing off the last of the french fries Zack had ordered as a midmorning snack. When Zack finished his memo, he buzzed Mrs. Gibbs.

"Mrs. Gibbs," he said when she entered, "please type this up for me."

Mrs. Gibbs took the memo, but she hesitated. "Mr. Morris—"

"Yes, Mrs. Gibbs, what is it?"

"Mr. Monza called again from the basement. He wanted to remind you again that he needs authorization to buy those electricity thingies."

"Right, Mrs. Gibbs." Zack nodded. "I always say that I can't do a thing without thingies."

"That's what Mr. Monza said," Mrs. Gibbs agreed, nodding her head rapidly like a bird digging for worms. "He says if he can't buy them, the new microwave ovens might blow a fuse. And they're being delivered to the home economics classes this morning. Now, all you have to do is sign that form there in triplicate and keep the carbon."

Zack stole back one of his french fries from Slater. "I'll get right on it, Mrs. Gibbs."

"And there's the nutrition study for the cafeteria food—here, I'll leave it right on your desk. I hope you've taken a look at the reorganization plan for the clerical staff. Oh, and there are a number of students waiting to be disciplined, Mr. Morris."

"Right," Zack said. "Tell them to wait in the cafeteria."

"The cafeteria, Mr. Morris?"

"As long as they have to wait, they might as well eat," Zack said. "Now, I have work to do." He waited until Mrs. Gibbs ran out, then turned to Slater. "Slater, don't you think you ought to get back to class?'' he prodded. "I think you've had enough. Forty minutes of soap operas is ample punishment for even a big guy like you.''

"I'll go in a minute,'' Slater said. His eyes were glued to the television set.

"Are you really into that show?'' Zack asked incredulously.

"No way,'' Slater said. He ate another french fry, still staring at the screen. "I'm just passing the time, that's all.''

Zack leaned over and picked up the microphone for the PA system. He thought a minute, then pressed the button. "Students, this is your principal speaking. Thought for the day: It's never too late to slack off. Another message from the Zack Morris philosophy. Xeroxed copies will be available after school at the school store for fifty cents.'' He pushed the microphone back again and made a note to have Screech help him out with the Zack Morris philosophy book.

Slater gave him an irritated look and returned his attention to the television. "Can't you be quiet for a minute? I want to see if Trent Steed gets his kidney transplant.''

"But you're not into the show or anything,'' Zack said.

"No way,'' Slater said again, eating another fry. "It's just that Lisa hasn't told Trent that he's really Chandler Van Cormandt's son. He doesn't know that he's getting Chandler's kidney. Chandler's his sworn enemy, and—"

"Okay, okay," Zack said. "You can stay another five minutes."

Mrs. Gibbs knocked and came in. She handed Zack a typed piece of paper. "Here's your memo, Mr. Morris."

Zack thanked her, then waited until she'd left to pick up the microphone to the PA system. "Cody Durant, please report to the principal's office," he intoned. He grinned as he released the button. Watch out, surfer boy. Principal Morris's plan was in motion at last!

Chapter 3

Over in the chemistry lab, things were not going as fabulously as Lisa had thought they would. She'd stayed up late last night, trying to think of the perfect topic for her lecture. And she'd finally come up with one she thought was ideal: The Magic World of Blush. What could be better than seeing the practical uses of chemistry?

But the class didn't seem interested in the array of products she'd brought in. Not the gels, not the creams—not even the powders! Even the newest shade she'd purchased, Overripe Apricot, only got one giant yawn. It spread like the wave at a Tiger football game from Tony Berlando in the first row all the way back to Binky Grayson in the last.

Finally, Lisa decided to do something drastic. She cleared her throat. "Screech," she called, "can you come up front and be a visual aid, please?"

Screech bobbed up immediately. "Of course, Miss Turtle," he said, and practically ran up the aisle to the front of the room in his purple high tops and red pants.

"Pay attention, class. This will be a challenge," Lisa said cheerfully as she sat Screech in a chair facing the class. She scrutinized Screech's face while he blinked at her adoringly. "Screech has undertones of green in his complexion," she announced.

"Green?" Screech squeaked. "My face hasn't been green since I ate five enchiladas in a row at Mel's House of Tamales."

"Take it from me, Screech, it's green," Lisa declared. She scanned her row of products. "You just need something to warm it up."

"How about another enchilada?" Binky yelled from the back row.

Lisa glared at Binky disapprovingly. "That's enough, Binky. Pay attention, and you just might learn something."

"About blush? Who cares?" Binky muttered. Lisa ignored the titters from the class.

She swooshed her brush over the blush several times. "This is Perfect Peach," she explained. "Now, just watch how it warms up Screech's skin tone."

She dusted the powder on Screech's cheekbones.

"Perfect!" Lisa said. She handed him a mirror and let Screech admire himself.

"Very nice, Lisa." Screech nodded approvingly. "It brings out the green in my eyes, too."

Stocky Butch Henderson, who was a fullback on the football team, slammed his book shut. Everyone jumped. Lisa peered at the class anxiously, hoping she wouldn't have a riot on her hands.

Butch heaved a huge sigh and stood up. "This is totally bogus," he said. "I could care less about bringing out the peach in my skin tone." He started down the aisle toward the rear door.

Tony Berlando stood up, too. "You said it."

Daisy Tyler tried to shush them. "*I* care," she pouted.

"This is worse than real chemistry," Jeremy Frears groaned. "Isn't it, Greg?"

He elbowed his best friend, but Greg Tolan was fast asleep.

Lisa's dark eyes filled with tears. Everybody hated her lecture. She was a complete and utter failure! Mr. Trapezi, the chemistry teacher, had fallen asleep long ago in the back row. At least he didn't wake up and see what a miserable job she was doing. It was *hard* to keep a class's attention, Lisa realized.

Screech turned and saw the tears in Lisa's lovely dark eyes. He had to help her. He sprang up immediately. "I have an idea!" he exclaimed. "I'll show the class my newest chemistry experiment!"

Butch stopped on his way down the aisle. "Well, it's gotta be better than blush," he said, and returned reluctantly to his seat.

Lisa blinked back her tears and watched Screech gratefully as he quickly gathered up the ingredients he needed. Within moments, he had the experiment set up at a front lab desk.

Screech cleared his throat. He held up a tube of clear liquid. "Now, class," he announced, "if I add this liquid to this powder, you'll see something amazing." Actually, Screech had only tried this once. If he was right, the class would see the mixture slowly turn into beautiful crystals. Then he could give one to Lisa as a present. That should make her feel better.

"Okay, watch carefully." Screech poured some of the liquid into the beaker full of powder. The liquid began to bubble. So far so good. But in another moment, the mixture began to smoke. Startled, Screech reached for the beaker and knocked it over. It quickly knocked over the tube with the rest of the liquid, which spilled on the extra powder. The whole mess went up in a tiny explosion. Smoke billowed out and began to fill the room.

"That *was* amazing," Butch said. "I can't see *anything*."

"I'm out of here," Tony said, coughing.

"Take me with you!" Daisy squealed. "I'm scared!"

Lisa could hear the sounds of a frantic exit. Chairs were scraped, books were dropped, and footsteps thundered toward the front and back doors of the lab. But her eyes were tearing, and she couldn't see a thing.

"Screech?" Lisa felt through the smoke for Screech. "Are you still there?"

"I'm here," Screech said. He felt Lisa touch his shoulder, and he nearly fainted with happiness.

"We'd better get out of here," Lisa said nervously. "My mascara isn't waterproof."

"Follow me," Screech ordered masterfully. He grabbed Lisa's hand and inched his way through the smoke toward the door. But halfway there, he stopped. "The mice!" he cried.

▲   ▼   ▲

"Okay, Slater," Zack said. "Your time is up. Back to class."

"But I just ordered nachos from the Max!" Slater complained.

Zack jerked his thumb toward the door. "Out!"

Slater leaned over the desk. He looked very large and very strong. "You know, preppie," he said menacingly, "Tomorrow you won't be able to order me around."

"I've still got four hours to go," Zack said, unconcerned. He knew Slater's bark was worse than his bite. Underneath those muscles beat the sweetest heart in the world. Not that Zack would ever admit that to anyone, especially Slater. Slater would probably break his face, and it would ruin his own cool image.

"Okay, okay," Slater grumbled. He picked up his books. "I'll see if I can get into some more trouble. 'All My Transgressions' is coming on. Don't eat my nachos, man."

On the way out, Slater almost bumped into Mrs. Gibbs, who was scurrying in. "Mr. Morris, that authorization—"

"Yes, Mrs. Gibbs. I just need to take care of one thing first," Zack told her.

"You mean thingie?" Mrs. Gibbs asked hopefully.

"No, *thing*," Zack repeated. "I'll take care of the thingies right after the thing." He shook his head, confused. "I think."

Just then, Cody Durant knocked on the open door. With a despairing glance at Zack, Mrs. Gibbs went out.

Cody Durant walked into the office, looking like Mr. September in a calendar of Hot Guys. Zack's heart sank all the way into his high tops. The girls were right—the guy was gorgeous.

"Hi," Cody said. "I have to admit, this is kind of cool, to walk into the principal's office and see a guy like me."

Fat chance, Zack thought sourly. He considered himself good-looking, but he had to admit that Cody was in another league.

"What a day to start at a new school," Cody continued with an easygoing grin. "Wacky doesn't begin to cover it."

If Zack wasn't careful, he'd start *liking* this character. Cody seemed like a pretty good guy. Then Zack thought of Cody kissing Kelly, and things shifted back into the proper perspective. The guy was a snake.

"This isn't a game, Mr. Durant," Zack said gravely. "Here at Bayside High, we're serious about, uh, Wacky Wednesday. Please sit down."

Cody looked abashed. "Sorry," he said. "I didn't mean to be rude or anything."

Zack stared at the paper in his hand. "Can you tell me, Mr. Durant, why you were in study hall when you should have been in social studies?"

Cody looked puzzled. "But I *was* supposed to be in study hall. I'm in all Kelly Kapowski's classes. And I'm not complaining about it in the least," he added with a delighted grin. The grin immediately collapsed when he saw Zack's expression. "What was your name again?" Cody asked tentatively.

"Morris," Zack said tersely.

"Not *Zack* Morris?" Cody asked. "Kelly's old boyfriend?"

Zack nodded once.

"Oh, man." Cody ran a hand through his thick black hair. "Sorry. I know you and Kelly were tight. She told me all about it. But she says that you're just friends now, right?"

Zack nodded again.

"So you won't mind if I date her, then?" Cody asked. Zack didn't nod. "Look, I'm new here. The only waves I want to make are at the beach. So tell me, man to man, if you have a claim here."

For one brief, insane moment, Zack considered telling the truth. But if he told Cody to back off, Kelly would find out. It was just the sort of thing that would infuriate Kelly, having two boys discuss who had a claim on her. *What am I, a mine?* she'd yell, her blue eyes icy with fury. Then she'd dump both of them.

And besides, it might not work.

Zack shuffled some papers. "Not that I think this conversation is appropriate, Mr. Durant. But, no, I don't have a claim on Kelly. You're free to proceed."

Cody's grin was as easygoing as always. "Cool.

Because I probably would have, anyway. What guy would be crazy enough to let Kelly get away?"

You're looking at him, Zack thought. Cody was right. Zack was so crazy he should be committed. "Back to the matter at hand, Mr. Durant," he said tightly. It was time to exert some major principal muscle.

Zack rose and whipped the paper in front of Cody's face. "Is this your name?" he asked, pointing to the top.

"Yes."

"And is this a class schedule?"

Cody stared at the paper. "It looks like it. But—"

"And does this say social studies?" Zack asked, pointing.

"Well, yeah. But—"

"I rest my case!" Zack finished.

Cody shook his head while he stared at the paper. "I guess there was some sort of mixup."

"We refer to it as cutting class, Mr. Durant," Zack said, frowning. "And we take it very seriously at Bayside High."

"But I didn't cut it. I didn't *know* about it!" Cody protested. "Mr. Belding gave me—"

"I'm the principal right now, Mr. Durant. And I think detention is in order after school today. Now, please proceed to Mr. Testaverde's class."

Cody got up, shaking his head. He looked at the

schedule again, then shrugged. "Well, okay, I guess. Thanks, Mr. Morris." Still puzzled, he walked out.

"All *right!*" Zack exclaimed, as soon as the door had closed behind Cody. He could spirit Kelly away right after school. He'd take her for a ride to the beach and they'd watch the sunset. Then, he could move in. Even if Kelly was undecided, Zack had a feeling that he could win her over in a few days. After Terrible Testaverde found out that Cody had cut his class, he'd give him enough penalty assignments to keep him busy for days! Zack would have a clear field. And he could begin that mature, honest relationship with Kelly.

Zack's daydreaming was interrupted by a series of sharp raps at his door. By this time, he recognized Mrs. Gibbs's nervous knocking.

"Yes, Mrs. Gibbs—the thingies," he called out. "I'm getting right—"

Mrs. Gibbs poked her head in. "No, Principal Morris. It's something else. You *must* discipline this student. He has completely disrupted second-period study hall. He let loose a whole bunch of mice, and all the students ran out screaming. The entire second floor is in chaos! Students and mice are running everywhere!"

Zack frowned. Who could the troublemaker be? He knew where *he* was, so it couldn't be him. Maybe it was one of the senior hoods, like Denny

Vane. Denny was about six foot five, and Zack wasn't crazy about having to discipline him. Too bad he'd kicked Slater out. It would be nice to have some muscle standing behind him when he gave Denny detention.

"Okay, Mrs. Gibbs," he agreed. "Send the troublemaker in."

Mrs. Gibbs nodded rapidly and ran out. In another moment, Mr. Belding walked in. His orange baseball cap was awry, and he looked stricken.

"It wasn't my fault!" he exclaimed.

Chapter 4

Talk about discipline! It was the hardest thing in the world for Zack to control his glee. Mr. Belding was at his mercy! He wanted to burst out laughing.

Instead of laughing, he frowned. It made him want to laugh even more, so he deepened the frown until he thought his face would crack. "Mr. Belding," he intoned, "I am not interested in whose fault it was at the moment. Why don't you tell me exactly what happened." Having been reprimanded by Mr. Belding a million times sure came in handy, Zack thought triumphantly. He had the rap down perfectly.

"Nothing happened!" Mr. Belding began.

What a perfect cue! "Do you mean Mrs. Gibbs brought you here for *nothing*?" Zack asked. "Do you call students running all over the second floor being chased by mice *nothing*? Well, I call that something, mister, and you'd better start explaining!"

"All I did," Mr. Belding burbled, "was get up to ask Brenda a question—"

"Do you mean Ms. Dickerson?" Zack asked pointedly. "Since when do we address teachers by their first names at Bayside High, Mr. Belding?"

"Ms. *Dickerson*," Mr. Belding responded tightly. Zack could tell that Mr. Belding was starting to get irritated with him. But Mr. Belding would rather die than step out of his role as a student. Wacky Wednesday had been his idea, and he had to follow through.

"And what did you want to ask Ms. Dickerson?" Zack prodded.

Mr. Belding blushed. "It's not important," he mumbled.

Another cue. Zack rapped on his desk. "I'll decide what's important, Mr. Belding."

"I wanted to know if I could go to the bathroom," Mr. Belding muttered. He gave Zack the evil eye.

Zack suppressed a smile. He should win an Oscar for this role. Best Performance as a Leading Male Impersonating an Authority Figure. "Proceed," Zack said.

"So I got up and started down the aisle and there was this sort of corral made of ice-cream sticks—"

Uh-oh, Zack thought. *Screech.*

"—only I didn't see it. I tripped over it, and all the mice got out," Mr. Belding finished. "The next thing I knew Phyllis Ptowski had jumped into my arms. The rest of the girls ran out screaming." He felt his back gingerly.

Phyllis Ptowski was pretty plump, Zack thought sympathetically.

"My back will never be the same," Mr. Belding muttered.

Zack frowned. "This is very serious, Mr. Belding. I'm shocked—shocked!—that a student of your caliber would play with mice."

"I didn't play with them!" Mr. Belding roared.

"Don't raise your voice to the principal, mister, or you'll be sorry," Zack answered calmly. "And you *will* be sorry." He buzzed for Mrs. Gibbs. When she came in, he said, "Mrs. Gibbs, please take this student to detention. Lock him in and throw away the key!"

"But—" Mrs. Gibbs said.

"Zack!" Mr. Belding protested. He looked as though he wanted to jump over the desk and strangle him.

Zack held up a hand. "Principal Morris, if you please. Is this Wacky Wednesday or not?" He smiled at Mr. Belding. "I'm learning so much," he assured him.

"I'm so glad," Mr. Belding said through clenched teeth. Then Mrs. Gibbs grabbed him by the arm and hauled him out.

Zack tilted his chair back and leaned against the wall. He was learning the delicate balance between freedom and discipline, just like Mr. Belding had said. He was getting so good at it he thought it was time to discipline another student. Zack leaned over and pressed the button to activate the PA microphone.

"Miss Kapowski, please report to the principal's office," he intoned.

▲   ▼   ▲

When Kelly walked in, Zack wondered if he'd made a mistake. Maybe he should have waited a while before summoning Kelly. She looked steaming mad, and he had a feeling he knew the reason why. She stood in the middle of his office, her hands on her hips, looking gorgeous in a rose pink mini-skirt and matching flowered T-shirt. He just wanted to grab her and kiss her. But the look in her eye was not exactly come-hither.

"Zack Morris, just what are you up to?" Kelly exploded, her hands still on her hips.

"That's *Principal* Morris to you," Zack tried.

"Don't give me that," Kelly shot back. "You're not a principal, you're an underhanded, unprincipled . . . *meathead*!"

"Meathead?" Zack asked.

"Meathead," Kelly repeated.

Zack tried one more time to tread the fine line between freedom and discipline. He wore his deepest frown. "Miss Kapowski, do you know I could send you to detention for calling your principal a meathead?"

"Go ahead," Kelly said craftily. She tossed her gleaming hair behind one shoulder. "I'll spend it with Cody Durant."

Whoops. Maybe it was the wrong approach. Zack came around the desk and approached Kelly. "Now, Kelly," he cooed soothingly, "why don't you just calm down and tell me what's wrong."

"I won't calm down," Kelly said, "but I *will* tell you what's wrong, Zack Morris. I bumped into Cody. He told me that his class schedule was changed. Terrible Testaverde gave him a load of assignments. And *you* gave him detention for skipping class."

"But I had to," Zack answered, widening his hazel eyes to give Kelly his most sincere look. "That's my job, Kelly. It's hard, but—well, it had to be done."

"But *you* changed his class schedule!" Kelly pointed out.

"It was a—an administrative decision," Zack responded quickly. It sounded impressive, so he went on. "Scheduling is a delicate balance, Kelly. Freedom and discipline, you know. It's very complicated and hard to explain if you don't have the experience. Class loads, hall traffic, fire regulations—they all play a part." He patted Kelly's shoulder. "Maximum capacity, Kelly! It's the wave of the future."

"Zack, let me ask you something," Kelly said evenly. "Do you actually think I'm going to *buy* this?"

Zack gave her a scintillating smile. "Well . . . yeah."

"Forget it, buster," Kelly snarled. "You changed Cody's schedule so he wouldn't be in my classes. You put him in Testaverde's class so that he'd get buried with assignments. I've known you too long to be fooled. You're up to your old tricks."

"Kelly—"

"What I can't figure out," Kelly interrupted, "is why. Is this some kind of scheme to get me to date you again?"

Zack stared into Kelly's furious blue eyes. He knew that if he confessed, it would get their relationship off on the wrong foot. And it might prevent them from ever getting together at all. If Kelly knew that he was scheming and scamming to get her back, she'd be even more furious at him. She couldn't know it, Zack decided. He had to stick to his guns if he wanted a mature, honest relationship. He had to lie.

"No way, Kelly," he said, taking her hand. "Really. I know you and I are over. But that doesn't mean we're not friends, does it?"

"Of course not, Zack," Kelly said, confused. "We *are* friends. We always said that our friendship came first."

"Well, I did what I did because of our friendship, Kelly," Zack said, oozing sincerity. "It wasn't some dirty trick to get me what I want. It was an idea I had to protect *you*."

Kelly shook her head. "From what?"

Gently, Zack led Kelly to the couch. He brought her to sit down next to him. A delicate perfume wafted toward him from her hair or her skin, and it was enough to send his pulse racing.

"I know you, Kelly," he said softly. "I know that you're pretty much head over heels for Cody already. Aren't you?"

Kelly blushed. "Zack," she said uneasily, "I feel funny talking about this with you."

"But, Kelly, we *should* talk about it. It's important for our friendship," Zack said. "What kind of friends could we be if we couldn't discuss each other's boyfriends and girlfriends?"

"Girlfriends?" Kelly asked, surprised. "Are you seeing someone, Zack?"

Was that jealousy he saw lurking in her deep blue eyes? A tiny spurt of hope flared in Zack. All was not lost! "Not at the moment," Zack confessed.

"But if I *do* meet someone, I want to be able to talk to you about her. Honesty, Kelly. That's what friendship is all about."

Kelly nodded. "You're so right, Zack. Okay, I guess I am pretty much head over heels for Cody. I just can't believe how fantastic he is."

Zack had expected it. But it still didn't mean he liked *hearing* it. As a matter of fact, it really hurt. But he couldn't do what he wanted—get up and stomp around, cry, jump out a window—so he just squeezed her hand.

"Ow!" Kelly said.

"Oh, sorry," Zack apologized. "Now, back to Cody. I'm happy for you, Kelly. But I'm also concerned."

"But why?" Kelly asked. "I've never been happier."

Zack nodded. "Well, maybe. But it's so soon. I wouldn't want you to rush into anything. He hurt you once before, remember?"

"You mean when he didn't write to me," Kelly said in a subdued voice. "I know. But we talked about it, and it's okay."

"But it still hurt back then, didn't it?" Zack pressed her. "You spent a whole month together and then he went off and you never heard from him again."

Kelly's eyes were soft and wounded. "You're right," she admitted. "It hurt a lot."

"Then can't you see why I'm concerned?" Zack asked. "What if he hurts you again?"

"Zack, it's a risk I'll have to take," Kelly said. "You have to, if you fall in love."

Zack was feeling desperate. He wasn't getting through to Kelly at all. But at least she wasn't angry with him anymore. "Kelly, I'm sorry if I went too far," he said finally. "You have to believe I was only trying to protect you. I figured you needed time to test your feelings. If you're with Cody all the time, you won't be able to think straight."

"But that's *my* decision to make, Zack," Kelly said gently.

"You're absolutely right," Zack agreed. "Absolutely. It's just that you mean so much to me. I mean, your *friendship* means so much to me."

"Oh, Zack." Kelly's eyes were bright with a sheen of tears. "You're so sweet. Your friendship means a lot to me, too. I'd never want to lose it."

The moment was right. Well, maybe it wasn't perfect, Zack thought. It could be too soon. But Kelly looked so beautiful, so soft. She was gazing at him with such tenderness that he couldn't help himself. Her full lips parted slightly. Zack leaned forward. . . .

The door flew open and hit the wall with a bang. Slater ran in. "What are you doing sitting here talking to Kelly, Zack?" he demanded. "The whole school is falling apart!"

Chapter 5

Irritated, Zack looked up. "Slater, I'm in conference," he said pointedly.

"But the students are revolting!" Slater shouted in exasperation.

"So what else is new?" Zack said. "They've always been pretty gross."

Kelly stood up abruptly and Zack lost his balance, crashing to the floor at Kelly's feet. "What do you mean, Slater?" Kelly asked, concerned.

"Don't mind me, guys," Zack said from the floor. "I'm fine. Really."

"Somebody let loose all the laboratory mice," Slater told her. "They're running all over the second floor and spreading to the first. Girls are screaming and standing on desks. Mrs. Nolan jumped out a window."

"Oh, my gosh!" Kelly exclaimed.

"Luckily, she was on the first floor," Slater explained.

Kelly whirled around. "Zack, you have to do something—what are you doing on the floor?"

Zack sighed. "I'm having a very tiring day."

"Well, get up," Kelly ordered. "The situation is serious."

"It doesn't sound that bad," Zack said, leaning his head on his hand.

"On my way here, I passed the detention room," Slater went on. "It sounds like somebody is trying to break down the door."

Zack shrugged. "No problem. It's a strong door."

"The third floor is full of smoke from some sort of experiment Screech did in chemistry."

"No problem. I'll send someone to open some windows."

Slater put his hands on his hips. "Lisa set up a first-aid unit on the second floor so she could redo all the girls' makeup. But then the mice ran in. You can hear them screaming all the way in the other wing."

"The mice?" Zack asked.

Slater gave him an impatient look. "The girls."

Zack waved a hand. "No problem. They'll calm down."

"And over in home ec, Screech has decided to

make his marshmallow burritos. He's invited the entire floor to a party to taste them."

"No problem," Zack said with a yawn. "I'll call the nurse and make sure she has plenty of antacid."

Slater let out an exasperated breath. "And the football team has carted in a ton of dirt from the field and dumped it in the gym. They're turning the fire hose on it."

Zack's head slipped off his hand and his chin bumped the floor. He rubbed it. "Problem!" he groaned. He jackknifed to his feet. "The Mud-Wrestling Festival. I forgot to cancel it. Let's go."

"I just hope we're not too late," Kelly said worriedly as they raced out of the office.

"Me, too," Slater agreed. "I signed Jessie up for the first match, and I don't want to miss it."

▲   ▼   ▲

By the time Zack, Kelly, and Slater reached the gym, things were out of control. The football team had challenged the cheerleaders to a tug-of-war, and it appeared that the football team was winning. The burly linebackers and fullbacks hollered and grunted while the entire cheerleading squad, minus its captain, Kelly Kapowski, yelled and squealed as they slid closer and closer toward the dividing line.

The line, a bright red streamer held by students in opposite bleachers, trembled as the audience screamed and cheered. Daisy Tyler was first in line on the cheerleaders' side. Her face was bright red, and she shouted back at her team to stand fast. Even while she screamed victory, her white sneakers slid slowly in defeat toward the football team.

"This is awful," Kelly moaned. "The gym is a mess. And the cheerleaders are losing, too."

"Come on," Zack said. "I see Lisa and Jessie."

Zack, Kelly, and Slater made their way through the crowd to Lisa and Jessie, who were watching the commotion from the sidelines. Lisa was wearing a raincoat and was cheering on the cheerleaders with lusty yells. Jessie had her arms crossed and looked concerned.

Just then, beefy Butch Henderson gave a mighty yank, and Daisy Tyler was jerked through the streamer, breaking it. The rest of the cheerleaders went down in the mud like dominoes.

The cheers exploded into a deafening roar. The mud-splattered football team took a bow. Then a chant went up for the next event, a mud-wrestling competition between the cheerleaders.

Kelly turned to Zack. "You've got to do something."

"I know," Zack said, frowning. Even he had to admit that things were out of hand.

Jessie's pretty face was set in angry lines. "I won't let them do it," she muttered. "I won't." Suddenly, she ran over and hopped on the first row of bleachers. "Attention, everybody!" she yelled, and the gym slowly quieted a bit.

"Bayside High is a nonsexist institution!" she cried out ringingly, raising a fist. "We do not mud wrestle! It's disgusting and sexist!"

Slater sprang up. "I agree!" he shouted.

Jessie gave him a disbelieving look. "You do?" she asked hopefully.

Slater nodded, his brown eyes twinkling. "Absolutely." He turned to the rest of the gym. "I vote for a wet T-shirt contest instead!"

The guys in the gym began to pound on the bleachers. "Wet T-shirts! Wet T-shirts!"

Zack hurried to the middle of the gym, side-stepping mud-encrusted cheerleaders on the way. He held up a hand for quiet. Nobody shut up.

"Okay, everyone—" he shouted. But the words were hardly out of his mouth when the lights went out.

Zack groaned. What had gone wrong? Suddenly, he remembered the electricity thingies. Had Screech plugged in all the microwave ovens at once? He wouldn't be that stupid, would he? "Zack, you're talking about *Screech*," he muttered to himself.

Meanwhile, pandemonium had erupted in the gym. Girls were screaming, guys were yelling, and nobody could see a thing.

"Quiet, everyone!" Zack shouted, but his words were drowned out. He slid his way back over to where he'd been standing. "Kelly!" he shouted. "Are you okay?"

"I'm right here, Zack," Kelly said. He felt her soft hand on his arm. "And I'm fine. But this is getting out of control."

"Somebody could get hurt," Jessie said worriedly.

"I think it's time to be a principal, preppie," Slater advised. "You gotta control this crowd."

"I'll say," Lisa said in a disgusted tone. "I got mud all over my new pink playsuit. And I think I lost a contact."

"What can we do to help?" Jessie asked.

Zack's eyes were now adjusted to the dim light. Someone had turned on a radio, and some students were dancing in the mud. Someone jumped off the bleachers and landed in the mud, splattering it over a few cheerleaders who had just cleaned themselves off. They tackled the offender, and he went down with a dying scream.

"First of all, we have to kill that radio," Zack said. "Then I'll try to calm everyone down."

"Isn't there a megaphone in Coach Sonski's office?" Lisa asked.

Slater nodded. "I'll get it."

But before Slater could move, Screech burst into the gym, followed by all the home ec classes. At least Zack *thought* it was Screech. He certainly looked like their skinny, curly haired friend. But his face was covered with white sticky goo, and he was wearing a miner's helmet with a flashlight attached to it.

But then Screech's high-pitched voice came out of the sticky white face. "The microwaves exploded!" he said. "We made all the burritos and I'd even cut up the gherkin garnishes. I said, 'One, two, three, start cooking,' and boom!"

"Is that when the lights went out?" Zack asked.

Screech wiped the goo out of his eyes. "How'd you know? I had to stop by the prop room for the helmet so I could see. What's going on?"

Zack sighed. "I have to find Mr. Monza. We must have blown a major fuse."

"What about the Mud-Wrestling Festival? We'll need some candles," Screech observed. He scraped some marshmallow off the front of his shirt. "I can provide the hors d'oeuvres."

Butch Henderson overheard Screech and shouted, "Candlelit mud wrestling!"

An answering cry from the football team started up across the gym. "Mud wrestling!"

Butch grabbed Kelly by the waist and hoisted her into the air. "First, Kelly Kapowski versus Daisy Tyler!"

"Put me down, Butch!" Kelly yelled.

Zack decided it was time to step in, even if Butch did weigh fifty pounds more than he did. "Butch, put Kelly down!" he ordered, and just then the lights went back on. Butch turned and looked him dead in the eye. "Uh, please?"

Behind Butch and Kelly, the door opened again. This time, Mrs. Gibbs scurried in, followed by a well-dressed group. The women were in silk dresses and suits, and the men were all wearing ties. All of them wore dazed expressions as they glanced around at the pandemonium.

Mrs. Gibbs sidled up to Zack. "It's the school board," she hissed. "They've come to make their surprise inspection for the Principal of the Year Award. I can't find Mr. Belding anywhere!"

A tall, angular woman stepped forward. Her thin lips pressed together as she squinted around in the gloom. "What is going on here?" she demanded. "Who is in charge?"

Mrs. Gibbs whispered to Zack, "It's the head of the school board, Mrs. Fingerman."

"Who is responsible for this chaos?" Mrs. Fingerman repeated furiously. "Is this a high school or a clown school? Where is Mr. Belding? This is highly irresponsible!"

Zack stepped forward. "Mrs. Fingerman, you don't understand. Mr. Belding is a sober, respectable, highly *responsible* person. He—"

But Zack didn't get a chance to finish his sentence. The sober, respectable, highly responsible Mr. Belding suddenly burst into the gym through the opposite door. His hair stuck out of his baseball cap, his shirttails were flying, and he was covered in marshmallow goo. He was clutching the leg of a desk chair, his lips drawn back in a snarl.

Through the gloom, he caught sight of Zack. "Ban-*zai!*"

With an agonized yell, Mr. Belding sprang toward Zack. But the yell turned into a yelp as he slipped in the mud and slid, still screaming, into the school board. Mrs. Fingerman was the last to fall. She landed right on top of Mr. Belding.

Mr. Belding stared up into her face. He tentatively reached out and rubbed some mud off her face. "Oh, Mrs. Fingerman," he said. "How delightful to see you again."

Zack had a sinking feeling he was in big trouble. He scraped a bit of marshmallow off Screech's shirt. "Hors d'oeuvres, anyone?" he asked.

Chapter 6

The next morning, Zack leaned on his broom and surveyed the gym floor. "You haven't lived," he muttered, "until you've cleaned up marshmallow mud."

Zack had been working with the maintenance staff since seven-thirty that morning, and the gym was just starting to look clean. The mud had dried, but it was still a messy job to sweep it into piles and then shovel it into garbage bags.

Mr. Monza graciously had accepted Zack's offer of help after Mr. Belding had ordered Zack to offer. But Zack had a feeling that Mr. Monza wished Zack had stayed home. Maybe it was because he couldn't quite get the hang of how much dirt a garbage bag could hold without breaking. But was it his fault that when that last bag burst,

Mr. Monza happened to be standing nearby in his clean coveralls?

Across the gym, Mr. Monza looked at his watch. "You'd better get cleaned up, Zack. The bell is about to ring."

"Are you sure you don't want me to stay?" Zack asked. He felt guilty leaving Mr. Monza with the rest of the work. After all, it was Zack's fault that, instead of a gym, Bayside High had suddenly gained a new playing field. Mr. Monza had debated before they started whether they should sweep the floor or plant corn. "Because I've got one more bag to fill here—" Zack said, gesturing at an unused garbage bag.

Mr. Monza looked down at his formerly clean coveralls and winced. "No, really, Zack," he said hastily, "I can handle it from here." His mustache and wiry eyebrows twitched nervously.

Zack shrugged. "Well, okay."

He handed over his broom and went to wash up before heading outside to find the gang. He had tried to call Kelly last night, but one of her little brothers had said she was out and then banged down the phone. Zack was hanging on to a slender hope that Kelly hadn't been out on a date with Cody. Mr. Belding had canceled all detentions and punishments, so Cody would have had plenty of time to spend with Kelly. But there were lots of other things Kelly could have been doing last night,

Zack reassured himself. She could have been study-ing at the library, working out at the health club, or playing miniature golf. . . .

When he walked out onto the grassy quad, Jes-sie, Slater, Screech, and Lisa were all standing un-derneath the big elm tree, but there was no sign of Kelly.

"How was cleanup duty?" Jessie asked, her hazel eyes full of sympathy.

"Messy," Zack said with a grimace.

"Sorry Mr. Belding wouldn't let us help you," Lisa put in. "We did offer."

"I know," Zack said. "And I know it was the ultimate sacrifice for you, Lisa."

Lisa's big brown eyes widened. "No way," she assured him. "I've already made my ultimate sacri-fice. I had to give up mascara when I had that eye infection last spring." She shuddered. "It was awful."

"Well, forbidding us to help out was Mr. Beld-ing's last act as principal," Slater said ruefully.

Surprised, Zack looked at him. "What do you mean?"

"Did you hear something, Slater?" Jessie prompted.

"Tell us," Lisa urged.

"Mr. Belding has been suspended from school," Slater told them.

Zack whistled. "I know what *that's* like."

"I heard that, too," Screech said. "Actually, I hid in the air-conditioning duct during the meeting in Mr. Belding's office. The board told him he was a disgrace to Bayside High and that his taste in food was appalling."

"His taste in food?" Jessie asked, puzzled.

"Mrs. Fingerman sat on a plate of leftover nachos," Screech explained.

"Oops," Slater said. "I think that was my fault. I forgot all about them. Hey, are there any left?"

"Finally, something that isn't *my* fault," Zack said ruefully.

"I heard that we're getting an acting principal," Slater said. One corner of his mouth curled in disgust, as if nobody could replace Mr. Belding.

"An acting principal!" Screech exclaimed. "Cool! I like theatrical types."

Lisa rolled her big dark eyes. "He means a temporary principal, you goon."

"This is terrible," Jessie exclaimed. "Mr. Belding suspended? We have to do something."

"Right," Zack agreed. "We should all put our heads together." He was finally able to ask the question he'd been dying to ask since he arrived. "We need Kelly for this. Where is she?"

"She's probably still recuperating from her date with Cody last night," Jessie said dreamily, winding a brown curl around her finger.

Lisa gave a deep sigh. "Probably."

"What's with you two?" Slater asked, annoyed. "This guy isn't Mel Gibson, you know."

"But he's *close!*" Jessie and Lisa said at the same time. Then they burst into giggles.

"He's not close," Kelly said, coming up behind them. "He's better." Her blue eyes shone with a secret happiness, and she was hugging her books against her chest as though they were Cody himself.

Zack felt a deep pang in his heart that was worse than the most painful toothache he'd ever had. Kelly looked so beautiful and so in love. Had she looked so in love when they were together? He wondered. Why hadn't he committed how she'd looked to memory? At least he'd have something.

"Whoa, settle down, girl," Slater joked to Kelly. "You just might fly away if you're not careful."

"I wouldn't mind," Kelly said, "as long as Cody was with me."

Zack wanted to punch a tree, but instead he plastered a smile on his face. "I'm really happy for you, Kelly," he said.

He was rewarded with a dazzling smile. "Are you really, Zack? Thanks."

The bell rang, and the usual grumbling and gathering of books began. The gang made their way to the school building, but Zack trailed after the others, staring in a melancholy way at the back of

Kelly's long, shiny hair. Then, out of the corner of his eye, he saw someone approach. A Mel Gibson lookalike with sparkling green eyes and shaggy black hair.

"Guess who," Slater muttered under his breath.

"Mr. Wonderful," Zack snarled.

"Cody!" Kelly glowed as Cody swung into step beside her.

"Hi," Cody greeted her. Zack moved closer to hear their exchange. Cody leaned close to Kelly's ear. "I couldn't sleep last night. I just thought about you."

"Me, too," Kelly murmured.

Zack wondered if he could break into their conversation with the news that Kelly had a terrible contagious skin disease. But maybe it wasn't a good time.

He was saved, not by the bell, but by a whistle. A piercing, earsplitting whistle that made kids put their hands over their ears and stop in their tracks.

Zack looked over at the school steps. A burly woman in a khaki pantsuit was standing there, the whistle in her mouth. Even though she was short, something about the way she was standing commanded attention. Or maybe it was the baseball bat in her hand. She slammed it three times against the oak door to the school.

"Ten-*hut!*" she shouted.

The students turned and looked at each other. Daisy Tyler giggled. Rhonda Robustelli guffawed. Binky Grayson blinked.

"Uh-oh," Slater muttered. "This doesn't look good."

Next to Kelly, Cody Durant snapped to attention, as though it were a reflex, and his hand went up in a crisp salute. Zack could have sworn he clicked his heels together, but Cody was wearing sneakers so Zack couldn't hear anything. Kelly looked at Cody in amazement.

The woman on the front steps saw Cody and pointed at him. "There!" she said commandingly. "There is a student who knows discipline. At ease," she told Cody. She even gave him a thin smile of approval.

Cody struck the at-ease position. "I went to military school for a year," he muttered to Kelly. "It's a reflex."

The woman started down the stairs. "Ten-*hut!*" she shouted again, and this time the whole student body snapped to attention.

"My name is Ms. Martinet," the woman announced. "I've been appointed your temporary principal until Mr. Belding's appalling lapse of discipline can be investigated and the suitable punishment devised."

"But it wasn't Mr. Belding's fault," Jessie protested.

Ms. Martinet approached. She stood in front of Jessie. "Name," she rapped out.

"Jessie," Jessie said, defiantly tossing her curly mane of hair. Her hazel eyes flashed. She didn't deal with authority figures very well. Jessie didn't like being intimidated.

Ms. Martinet slammed the bat against the concrete, and Jessie jumped. Screech jumped behind Lisa and peeked over her head at the scene.

"Last name!" Ms. Martinet barked.

"Spano," Jessie practically whispered.

"Spano, half an hour detention for talking out of turn."

"But—"

"Make that one hour! Anybody else?" Ms. Martinet asked, spinning around and fixing every student with an icy gray stare. "Rule number one: No talking after the first bell. Rule number two: Silence must be maintained in the halls at all times. Rule number three: No miniskirts."

A groan went up among the male population, but it was stifled when Ms. Martinet whirled around. "Anybody else want detention?" she snapped. When no one spoke, she turned around again.

"Ms. Martinet, we abolished the dress code at Bayside High ten years ago," Slater pointed out. His voice rang out clear and strong, and Jessie looked at him, impressed.

"Are you crazy, man?" Zack muttered under his breath.

"Crazy like a fox," Slater said out of the corner of his mouth.

Ms. Martinet slowly turned until she saw Slater. She faced him without blinking. "Name."

"Slater, A. C."

"Detention, one hour. Today," Ms. Martinet said crisply. Then she blew her whistle and turned to the crowd. "March! One, two, one, two, one, two . . ."

As they marched toward the entrance, Jessie turned to Slater. "Why did you speak up like that?"

Slater shrugged. "She's wrong. I had to point it out even if it meant I got punished. Some things are worth it."

"I didn't think you had it in you, Slater," Jessie said approvingly.

"See you in detention, momma," Slater responded. Over his shoulder, he gave Zack a wink.

So, Zack thought, Slater was ready to make peace with Jessie. Getting stuck in detention together was the first step. There was nothing like mutual incarceration to provoke those tender feelings, Zack mused. But he'd already used that trick with Kelly junior year. He'd need another way to recapture his lost love. Besides, Kelly almost never got sent to detention. She was too good.

What a week, Zack thought tiredly as he made

his way to homeroom. Wacky Wednesday had been a disaster. He was a big enough man to admit it. He'd lost Kelly to a guy who looked like a movie star. Mr. Belding had been suspended and replaced by a former marine corps sergeant. Not only that, he had to spend his lunch hour today cleaning up the exploded marshmallow in the home ec room. Things couldn't get much worse.

▲   ▼   ▲

The PA system buzzed with static. Then Ms. Martinet's clipped voice came over the loud-speaker. "Good morning, Bayside High. This is Ms. Martinet, your principal. I have a few announcements."

Everyone in homeroom exchanged worried glances. What next?

"First item: It has come to my attention that there is a dance with a live rock band this Friday night in the gym. This is unacceptable after the events of yesterday. The dance is hereby can-celed."

Everyone in homeroom groaned. A few people turned to look at Zack as though it were his fault. Well, he guessed it was, in a way.

"No reactions, please," Ms. Martinet snapped, as if she could hear them. "Second item: the Senior

Picnic. Canceled. After yesterday's events, it is obvious that the seniors cannot be trusted to act in a mature fashion."

More groans. More students shot Zack dirty looks. He sank lower in his chair.

"Discipline in this school is deplorable," Ms. Martinet continued. "Starting today, we must rededicate ourselves to the grand ideal. The well-run school is a disciplined school. Remember Martinet's rules of order, or the four D's: Discipline. Diligence. Dedication. Destiny!" she concluded in a thrilling tone. Then the PA system buzzed and went dead.

Zack groaned and let his head fall into his hands. "She forgot a D," he said. "Depression."

Butch Henderson rose and stood over him, blocking out the light. "Thanks a lot, Morris," he said menacingly.

"Yeah," Vivian Mahoney said. "This is all your fault."

"No dance on Friday," Kelly murmured.

"No Senior Picnic!" Lisa wailed. "I've already bought my outfit."

"It's all your fault, Zack Morris," Daisy Tyler said with a sniff.

Everyone turned around and stared at him. Butch slapped a fist into his other palm and eyed him balefully.

"I just thought of another D," Zack told everyone helpfully. "Dead meat."

Chapter 7

After school that day, Slater approached the detention room, happily whistling a tune. He had thought it all out, and he'd decided that all he and Jessie needed was some time alone. In front of the gang, they'd get caught up in who could score bigger by putting down the other with faster and funnier insults. Then, before he knew what was happening, he'd go too far and Jessie would be mad at him again.

Slater knew he probably should leave that stubborn, infuriating, exasperating girl alone for good. But then she'd zing him with one of her comebacks, her hazel eyes would gleam, she'd toss that incredible mass of curly hair, and he'd be lost. Like it or not, he was hooked.

He'd liked her ever since the first day he'd met

her, when he'd moved to Palisades and gone to
Bayside High for the first time. Slater's father was in
the military and so Slater had grown up all around
the world. He was used to being an outsider. But he
wasn't used to kids welcoming him with the warmth
that Jessie, Kelly, Screech, Lisa, and Zack had. Even
though the gang had known each other since they
were kids, they never made him feel left out. In the
beginning, he almost hadn't wanted to spoil his
friendship with the gang by pursuing Jessie. But it
was impossible to keep his distance.

If only they'd stop arguing long enough for him
to let her know how he felt. The only time Jessie
kept her mouth shut was when he kissed her.
Maybe that was the only way they could make up.
Slater figured that he was up to the task.

He opened the door to Room 217 and peered
inside. Jessie wasn't there yet. He ambled in and
chose a seat near the back of the classroom. When
he faced front, he saw that a message was on the
board: ATTENTION, DETENTION-EES! REPORT TO THE
AUDITORIUM BY ORDER OF MS. MARTINET.

Slater scowled. The auditorium was a little im-
personal for his taste. It was way too big to get any
kind of interpersonal relations going. But then
again, he thought with a grin, he should look at it as
a challenge. If he could mellow out Jessie Spano in
a huge, drafty hall, he could do it anywhere.

Slater gathered up his books and headed for the

auditorium. A seat in the very last row would be perfect, he decided. The balcony overhung the last rows, creating some nice shadows. He and Jessie could feel completely alone there.

Ahead of him, Slater saw some familiar curves in black jeans, boots, and a moss green sweater. Jessie. And she looked absolutely fantastic. Her hair was loose today, and it cascaded down her back.

Slater quickened his pace and caught up to her at the auditorium door. "Looks like we're both stuck with detention today," he said.

Jessie nodded. He could tell that he still wasn't forgiven for disrupting her class on Wednesday. But the ice was definitely beginning to melt.

"I still can't believe you stood up to Ms. Martinet today," she said.

Slater gave a modest shrug. "There *are* causes I believe in, Jessie," he said softly.

Bingo! The frosty look in Jessie's eyes melted even more. "I'm glad to hear that," she said. "I thought you were just out for yourself."

Slater looked hurt. "I stand up for my fellow man, too, Jessie," he said. "And woman," he added, giving her a meaningful look. "Especially if she looks like you, momma."

He thought it was a compliment, but you never knew how Jessie was going to react. And this time she didn't melt; she got frostier. "There you go again," she said in exasperation. "As soon as you say something that's halfway intelligent, you spoil it. Don't you ever stop thinking about girls, Slater?"

"Of course I do," Slater said, taking her hand and giving her a serious look. "Every night. When I'm asleep. I dream about them instead."

Jessie snatched her hand back. "Why do I bother?" she asked dramatically, rolling her eyes in disgust. She shouldered open the door and disappeared inside.

Slater paused to run a hand through his hair and straighten his shirt. He probably shouldn't have made a joke, but he didn't think Jessie was as angry as she looked. And he would have a whole long hour all alone with her to convince her it was time to make up.

Slater pushed open the door and blinked in surprise. The auditorium was jammed with students! Rows upon rows were filled with grumbling, groaning kids getting out their homework while Ms. Martinet stood on the stage with her baseball bat. He looked over the bobbing heads for Jessie and saw her slip into an empty seat in the first row next to Vivian Mahoney.

Slater groaned. The joke was on him, after all. He'd never get a chance to make up with Jessie now!

▲   ▼   ▲

School on Friday was even worse than on Thursday. Ms. Martinet announced that she was considering a proposal to dismantle all school clubs except for the Chess Club. She also announced a new club called the Future Members of ROTC, and urged everyone to join. And everybody still blamed Zack. He could barely walk down the hall without receiving muttered threats and dirty looks.

Zack's true friends stuck by him, though. Slater, Screech, Lisa, Jessie, and Kelly even ate lunch with him in the cafeteria. They ignored the occasional sandwich wrapper that sailed through the air and bounced off Zack's head. But finally, the girls couldn't take it anymore. They left hurriedly, saying that they had to change for gym class, which didn't start for a half hour.

"We've got so many buttons today," Jessie explained uneasily. "It's going to take a while to change."

Kelly and Lisa nodded. "We really have to run," Lisa added. "Bye, Zack!"

Zack watched the girls run off, relief on their faces from escaping the table of gloom. He sighed. "I have to save the situation somehow," he said gloomily to Slater as a balled-up paper bag landed on their table from across the room. "We just have to get rid of Ms. Martinet!"

"You said it, preppie," Slater agreed. "Either that, or you're going to need a bodyguard."

"I'll be happy to volunteer, Zack," Screech offered.

"Maybe she'll quit," Zack said hopefully.

Slater shook his head. "I grew up on army bases, guy. People like Ms. Martinet just don't quit."

Zack and Screech nodded glumly.

"The only person Ms. Martinet can stand in the whole school is Kelly's boyfriend," Slater pointed out. "Cody went to military school, and she says he's full of the four *D*'s."

"I'm sick of the four *D*'s," Zack groaned.

"I keep forgetting them," Screech said, confused. "What are they again?"

Slater's brown eyes twinkled. "How about . . . Delicious debutantes defy daddies!"

Zack laughed. "Wait a second . . . Debonair doormen dance divinely."

"Disobedient dalmations defoliate dogwood!" Screech crowed.

But as soon as the joke was over, the three were sunk in gloom again.

"There's only one person who can help us," Zack said. "And the last time I saw him, he said he never wanted to see my face again."

"Who's that, Zack?" Screech asked.

"Let me give you a hint," Zack said. "Think marshmallow. If there had been any chocolate around, he would have looked like a s'more."

Screech looked thoughtful, but Slater grimaced. "Belding."

Zack nodded. "We have to go see him. He's the only one who can save us."

"I'll bring the chocolate," Screech offered.

▲   ▼   ▲

That night, Zack lay on his bed and stared at the ceiling. "Friday night and I'm all alone," he announced to his empty bedroom. "It's a teen tragedy."

He could have met Slater after his wrestling practice and gone out for burgers. He could have gone to the movies with his parents. He could have watched Screech design a new terrarium for his pet lizard. But Zack had chosen to avoid such excitement and brood instead.

A soft knock on his door made him jump up. "Come in," he called, wondering if his parents had skipped the movie and rented a tape instead.

But he nearly passed out when Kelly walked into the room. She was wearing faded jeans and a deep blue sweater that matched her eyes. "Hi, Zack," she said softly. "The back door was open, so I just came on up."

"Hi," Zack gulped. Had Kelly come over to tell

him that she'd decided that Cody Durant was dog meat? *In your dreams, preppie,* Slater would say.

"I'm meeting Cody at the Max," Kelly said, crossing over and sitting on the bed next to him. "But I just had to come over here first. I haven't had a chance to talk to you alone since Wacky Wednesday." She turned and gazed at him. "I just wanted to tell you that it really means a lot to me that you're behind me and Cody. You're the best."

"Thanks, Kelly," Zack said modestly. "I mean, that's nice of you to say."

"Oh, but I really mean it," Kelly said sincerely. She put a hand on his knee for a second, and Zack felt as though he'd been burned through his jeans. "And I wanted to ask you a favor," she said.

"Anything, Kelly," Zack swore. He'd promise her anything if she'd just keep her hand on his leg.

Kelly's hand dropped, and she stood up and began to pace. "Ms. Martinet thinks Cody is the best thing since Desert Storm," she said worriedly. "He can't even walk past her office without her calling him in. And the other kids are starting to notice. They're calling him Teacher's Pet—actually, they're calling him Dictator's Pet—and nobody will even talk to him!"

Zack started to smile, but Kelly turned and so he quickly assumed a concerned expression. "Really? That's awful." And he didn't even have anything to do with it! Cody had dug his own Bayside High grave when he'd snapped to attention for Ms. Martinet. All *right!* "That's high school kids, Kelly," he said soberly. "Sadists in stonewash."

"The thing is, Zack, I thought you could help," Kelly said, leaning against his desk. "You know how people listen to you—"

But Zack already was shaking his head. "Kelly, haven't you noticed that I'm dead meat at school, too? Everybody blames me for getting Mr. Belding suspended."

Kelly waved a hand. "That will wear off, Zack. Anyway, the point is that Cody needs friends. I mean, he has me, but he's kind of nervous about hanging out with the gang because of you."

"Me?"

Kelly blushed. "Because we used to go out, Zack. Cody thinks it might be weird if we all hung out together. That's why he won't even eat with us in the cafeteria. I tried to tell him that there's nothing between you and me anymore, that you're totally behind me and Cody, but . . ." Kelly shrugged. "He's got this crazy idea that you want to kill him."

Zack laughed hollowly. "Funny," he said.

"So I was wondering if you could convince him that he's wrong." Kelly cocked her head and looked at him pleadingly. "Zack, you can convince anybody about anything."

How could he resist that look? "Sure," Zack said with a sigh. "I'll give it a try." Kelly clapped her hands together. "Oh, thank you, Zack." She ran toward him and kissed him lightly on the cheek. His senses were overwhelmed with silky hair, soft lips, baby powder, and perfume. And then she was saying good-bye and running out the door.

Zack flopped back on the bed again. "Total teen tragedy," he said.

▲   ▼   ▲

On Saturday afternoon, Zack picked up Slater and Screech and drove to Mr. Belding's house. The top was down on his '65 Mustang, a soft breeze was blowing, and the sun was shining in a clear blue sky. It was perfect beach weather, and he just hoped he would live to enjoy it.

"Okay, you guys," Zack said as he turned down Mr. Belding's street. "Here's the deal. If he goes for my throat, you go for his ankles. Do an illegal tackle, Slater. You're the captain of the football team and you know how. Whatever it takes."

"We'll protect you," Screech assured him. "And if we can't, let's hope Mrs. Belding is around."

But when they knocked on the front door of Mr. Belding's modest brick house, nobody answered. "Maybe we should have called first," Zack said worriedly. "But I knew if I called he'd tell me not to come over."

Slater stepped over to the side of the door and peered through the window. "I think I see something," he said. "There's this faint bluish light off in the distance. And a shadow. I think someone *is* home."

Zack hammered on the door more loudly. "Mr. Belding!" he yelled. "We know you're in there."

"We really need to talk to you, Mr. Belding," Slater shouted.

"You've won a new color TV!" Screech yelled through the keyhole.

In another moment, they heard muffled footsteps approach the door. A lock twisted, and the door slowly opened.

Mr. Belding blinked at them. He was wearing a T-shirt, sweatpants, and a blue terry-cloth bathrobe, the sash trailing behind him. A bag of potato chips was clutched in one hand, a root beer in the other. His hair was messy, and his eyes were dull.

"Mr. Belding?" Zack said, shocked.

Mr. Belding took a step forward, and Zack shrank back in alarm. "Zack!" he said dazedly. "Good to see you. And Slater and Screech. Come on in, boys. Want some potato chips? Sour cream and bacon."

"Sure," Slater said cautiously. This new, super-friendly Mr. Belding was scary.

"Come on back to the family room," Mr. Belding said, shuffling off down the hall in his sweat socks.

Zack, Slater, and Screech exchanged shrugs. It sure didn't look like Mr. Belding. It didn't sound like him. His voice was faint and flat, with none of the warm authority they remembered. But it was him, all right.

When they walked into the family room, a soap opera was on the television screen. Crumpled-up bags of potato chips and cheese crisps littered the area around the couch. Stacked cans of root beer made an aluminum sculpture in one corner, and the afghan thrown over the couch was littered with peanut shells.

The three boys stood nervously in the middle of the room. "How's Mrs. Belding?" Slater asked politely to break the ice.

Mr. Belding sat on the couch and reached for the remote control. "She went to get me more blank videotapes," he said, his eyes on the screen. "Darn. I missed the big scene between Lisa and Trent Steed."

"I didn't know soap operas were on Saturday afternoon," Zack said with a frown.

"I taped some so I could watch them again," Mr. Belding said, settling back on the couch.

"*Again?*" Zack blurted.

Slater sat down next to Mr. Belding. "So did Lisa tell Trent that Chandler is his father?"

Mr. Belding nodded. "But she hasn't told him about the kidney yet," he confided. "It's coming up.

I can rewind to the other scene if you want."

"Sure," Slater said, reaching into a bowl for a handful of peanuts. "What did Trent say when he found out?"

"Mr. Belding," Zack interrupted, with a poisonous glance at Slater, "we didn't come here to watch soap operas."

"That's too bad," Mr. Belding said. "Because right after this, I have Cynthia and Rod's wedding on 'All My Transgressions.' Of course there's a bomb threat in the chapel, and—"

"Mr. Belding!" Zack interrupted sternly. "This is serious. Bayside High is in trouble."

"We need you," Screech put in.

"Right," Mr. Belding said. His eyes had a glazed look, and he was concentrating on the TV screen.

"You see, they replaced you with this former marine corps sergeant," Zack explained. "And she's ruining the school. She canceled the dance this weekend, and—"

"Zack, could you move over just a little bit?" Mr. Belding interrupted. "Just to the right—there. Good. Belinda is about to break it off with Justin. It's about time, too."

Zack sank back on an ottoman. What was wrong with Mr. Belding? He had all the energy and interest of a rutabaga. And it was all Zack's fault. Without a job, Mr. Belding's self-esteem had taken a nosedive.

Zack had a horrible thought. Closing his eyes, he pictured Mr. Belding in five years. His bathrobe would be practically rotting, but he wouldn't change it. He'd be an enormous couch potato, watching TV, surrounded by piles of empty sour-cream-and-bacon-flavored potato chip packages reaching all the way to the ceiling. Crates of Cheez Whiz would be stacked against one wall. Zack could see him now, cracking up for good when Belinda leaves Vance to rekindle her lost romance with Justin. He'd burst into wails and jump out a window, leaving a trail of peanut shells behind him.

Zack shuddered, then stood up and switched off the TV. "Mr. Belding, you may not want to hear this, but you're going to have to. We need you. You can sit here and try to forget about Bayside High, but we haven't forgotten about you."

Mr. Belding said nothing. He just sat there, fingering his remote control.

"Mr. Belding," Zack prompted, "we need your help."

"The situation is desperate, man," Slater said.

Screech nodded. "And it's getting pretty serious, too."

Slowly, Mr. Belding raised the remote control and turned on the TV. "Wish I could help you boys," he said numbly. "But I can't miss sumo wrestling at four."

Zack sighed. "Come on, guys," he said. "There's

nothing else we can do here. We're just going to have to help ourselves."

▲   ▼   ▲

Later that afternoon at the beach, Zack had just caught a wave when a great idea burst into his head. He saw it all—a way to get rid of Miss Martinet, reinstate Mr. Belding, and clear his name. And best of all, Zack thought as he rode the wave into the beach, he'd get rid of Cody Durant at the very same time.

Chapter 8

Zack knew that Cody was a fanatic about surfing, so he dragged himself out of bed early Monday morning and drove down to the beach. There was nothing in life Zack hated more than getting up early, but some things were worth it.

The early morning sun was just beginning to chase away the fog as Zack sleepily trudged down the sand to the water's edge. Without sun, the ocean was the color of steel, with lacy froth curling along the edges of the waves. Even as he watched, the sun broke through a patch of fog and the water glinted green. It was going to be another beautiful day in Palisades, California.

Zack squinted at the line of surfers sitting on their boards at the surf line. He probably should have brought his board along this morning, but he just wasn't that dedicated. And who wanted to surf without girls in bikinis watching you? What a waste of time.

He spotted Cody among the surfers, wearing a sleeveless wet suit with shorts. He saw how powerful Cody's arms were as he twisted to lie down on the board and began to paddle toward shore with sure strokes. Zack sent up a prayer that his plan would work. If Cody found out Zack had tried to break up him and Kelly, Zack would have to take off for Tortuga.

But Kelly was worth it, he told himself as Cody reached shallow water and slid off his board. His green eyes crinkled in a friendly way when he saw Zack.

"Hey, Zack! I didn't know you came to the beach this early," Cody greeted him, tossing the wet hair out of his eyes. "Uh, is everything okay?"

"Sure. I wanted to catch you before school," Zack said.

"Cool. What's up?" Cody slung his board under his arm as if it were a toothpick, and they started across the sand together.

"Look, Cody, I've noticed what's been happening at school," Zack began. "Just because Ms. Martinet has taken a liking to you, the kids are blaming you. I know just how you feel, since I'm in the doghouse at the moment myself. Everybody blames me for getting Ms. Martinet as our principal in the first place."

"That's rough, man," Cody said sympathetically. "Very un-cool."

"The reason I came to see you is that I think I know a way to solve both our problems," Zack said.

Cody planted his board in the sand with a single thrust. He turned back to Zack. "I'm listening."

"All we have to do is get rid of Ms. Martinet," Zack said craftily. "Together."

Cody shook his head. "Us? Easier said than done, my man."

"Maybe not," Zack said. "Here's my plan. Ms. Martinet thinks you're the greatest, right? Let's use it. Become her student assistant. I have a very close relationship with her secretary, Mrs. Gibbs. I'm sure I could get you in."

Cody frowned. "Wait a second. Won't that make things worse?"

"Maybe at first," Zack agreed. "But in the long run, no. You'll be like a double agent. You'll observe what's going on and report to me. As soon as we know her weaknesses, I'll be able to think up a plan. I guarantee we'll get Ms. Martinet off our backs. Will you do it?"

Cody unzipped his wet suit and crossed his arms, thinking. Zack wished he had kept himself covered up. There was nothing like staring at perfectly developed pectoral muscles to make a guy lose his nerve.

"Okay," Cody said. "I'll do it."

"Great!" Zack clapped him on the shoulder

and felt hard muscle. "Now, there's just one little thing. . . ."

Cody already had lifted his surfboard out of the sand again. He turned back. "What?"

"Ms. Martinet doesn't approve of student dating," Zack said. "And she *especially* wouldn't approve of her assistant dating a student. She thinks it's bad for morale. So you might have to cool it with Kelly for the duration."

"Cool it with Kelly!" Cody exclaimed. "No way. I'm not going to stop seeing Kelly. I mean, she's gorgeous."

Zack winced, but he gave Cody his most sincere look. "Kelly adores Mr. Belding," he said. "She was crushed when he left. Anybody who gets him reinstated will be on her *A* list, for sure. Once that happens, we can tell her everything."

"Why can't I tell her now?" Cody asked stubbornly.

Zack shook his head. "It just wouldn't work. Look, Cody, you should know something about Kelly. She's the most honest, sincere girl in the world. And she's a terrible actress. If you told her the truth, she'd still be mooning after you. But if you *don't*, Kelly will be devastated. And that's good."

Cody looked confused. "That's good?"

"Ms. Martinet will see that you really broke up with Kelly," Zack said persuasively. "She'll see that you sacrificed something for the greater good of the school. And you'll win her confidence. It's just like a double agent in the movies, remember? They always set up a situation where the agent *seems* to sacrifice one of his own. Right?"

"Yeah, well, I don't go to movies much," Cody said.

"Imagine all the students at Bayside High in your debt," Zack said. He came closer and spoke close to Cody's ear. "You'll be a hero. I can see them now, hoisting you on their shoulders. Renaming the auditorium Cody Durant Hall. Putting your name in the school song. Chanting. I can hear it now. Co-*dy!* Co-*dy!* Co-*dy!*"

Cody's eyes held a faraway look. "Cool," he breathed.

"And Kelly. I'll tell her the whole story when the time comes," Zack assured him. "Can you imagine how *grateful* she'll be?"

"Cool," Cody said dreamily. "Okay, man. I'll do it!"

"Cool," Zack said.

▲   ▼   ▲

On Tuesday afternoon after school, Jessie ran into Kelly outside of Bayside High. Her friend was sitting on the grass, her chin in her hands. Her brilliant blue eyes were cloudy when she looked up at Jessie. She stared down at her sneakers again.

"Something wrong?" Jessie asked. She sat down next to Kelly and crossed her long legs.

"How could you tell?" Kelly asked, her lower lip trembling.

"Gee, I don't know," Jessie said. "Maybe it's the grass stains on your chin." Kelly didn't even smile, and Jessie leaned over and nudged Kelly in the side. "What is it, kiddo?" she asked softly.

"It's Cody," Kelly said. "All of a sudden, he's ignoring me. This morning, he wouldn't walk to class with me. Last night, he didn't call me like he usually does. And at lunch, he avoided me. I don't know what's wrong, Jessie!" Kelly cried. A tear slowly slid down her cheek.

"I think I know just how you feel," Jessie said gloomily.

Kelly sniffed. "Trouble with Slater again?"

Jessie nodded sadly, then shrugged. "But what else is new? Let's get back to Cody. When did this start?"

"Yesterday," Kelly said. "I left a present in his locker, and he didn't even say thanks. And he *loves* zinc oxide!"

"Yesterday was the day he started as Ms. Martinet's assistant," Jessie said thoughtfully.

Kelly looked at her. "That's right," she said slowly. "Do you think she had something to do with this?"

"Well, she does have that anti-dating policy," Jessie said doubtfully. "But it's not like anybody obeys it."

"But Cody is!" Kelly wailed. "How much could he have liked me if he's willing to give me up so fast?"

Jessie slipped her arm around Kelly's shoulders and gave her a bracing squeeze. "Don't worry, Kelly," she said. "I'll come up with a plan. If we get rid of Ms. Martinet, Cody will come back to you."

Kelly reached into the pocket of her blue corduroy jeans and pulled out a tissue. She blew her nose vigorously. "That's great, Jessie," she said. "But I'm not sure if I want him anymore."

Jessie's mouth quirked in a half smile. "Right," she said. "I believe you. Who needs the spineless weasel?"

"Exactly," Kelly said bleakly. "Too bad I want the weasel more than ever."

▲   ▼   ▲

Zack met Cody by his locker. "How's it going?" he asked as Cody reached into his locker for his denim jacket.

Cody sighed. "Okay, I guess. Ms. Martinet really likes my salute."

"So what is she like?" Zack asked, leaning against the locker next to Cody's.

Cody thought a minute. "Well, she's superorganized. She divides the day into fifteen-minute segments, then figures out how many segments she needs to complete a task. She's got a little timer on her desk." He shook his head. "It's really wild, man. She drinks her tea at exactly three-thirty-five. I know, because I have to bring it in to her. One package of sugar substitute. Two-point-five teaspoons of milk. Then I stir it twice." Cody lightly banged his head against his locker. "I can't take it, man."

Zack patted him on the shoulder. "It's only for a few more days."

Cody's eyes were bleak. "It's a drag hurting Kelly, too. Are you sure about this?"

Zack leaned in closer. "Co-*dy*, Co-*dy*, Co-*dy*," he chanted in a low tone. Cody began to nod in the same rhythm.

"Cool," he said.

"Cool," Zack answered. "Now it's time for phase two."

▲   ▼   ▲

On Wednesday afternoon after school, Zack skidded into the Max. Jessie, Slater, Screech, Lisa, and Kelly were already there. Jessie was leaning over the table, talking intently, while the rest of the gang listened.

Zack didn't wait to hear what new social program Jessie was rooting for. He slid into the booth next to her and announced, "I have a plan."

"Zack, Jessie is talking," Lisa told him pointedly.

"Sorry, Jessie," Zack said hurriedly, "but this is superimportant. I've come up with a way to drive Ms. Martinet out for good!"

"But—" Jessie said.

"I figured it out while I was talking to Cody," Zack went on, barely noticing Jessie's interruption. He gave Kelly a significant look. "I've been talking to him pretty often."

Kelly gave a wan smile. "Thanks, Zack. But to tell you the truth, you don't have to anymore."

"No sweat," Zack said smoothly. "Anyway, this great idea just came to me. And it's simple."

"Zack," Slater said seriously, "Jessie has a plan, too."

"I really think I've come up with something," Jessie said. "I think—"

"Jess, hold on," Zack interrupted excitedly. "Let the scam master handle it. Just listen. Cody has been telling me about how compulsive Ms. Martinet is about order. She's completely out of her mind! So I think we should get everyone to go completely wild on Friday. We'll have Cody disrupt her schedule, put three sugars in her tea instead of one, stuff like that. All the girls will wear miniskirts. Guys'll wear shorts. Kids will kiss in the halls. We'll sing and dance on the way to class. We'll make Bayside High the most disorganized school ever. Ms. Martinet will self-destruct!''

He looked around from face to face. Nobody looked very excited. But maybe they were just tired. Kelly's eyes were red rimmed, and Jessie was definitely subdued. Usually, she'd jump right in after hearing a plan of his, with ways to improve it.

Maybe it was time for the topper. "Meanwhile,'' Zack continued, "I'll pretend to be the secretary of the school board and call Mrs. Fingerman. I'll say the board has been scheduled to make its return visit on Friday. Everything will be set. When the board comes, the school will be in even worse chaos than on Wacky Wednesday!''

"Pardon me for interrupting,'' Jessie said coolly. "But how is this going to get Mr. Belding reinstated? What if the board decides that Bayside High needs an even *stronger* hand than Ms. Martinet's?''

Zack waved a hand in dismissal. "Jessie, who's the premier schemer here? My plan will work. Trust me.''

He stood up triumphantly. "I'll set the stage to-morrow. Remember, girls, spread the word: mini-skirts on Friday. The shorter the better."

"I think that's the only part of your plan I like," Slater grumbled.

Chapter 9

Zack made his plans. On Thursday afternoon after school, Cody was scheduled to work for an hour and a half in Ms. Martinet's office. Zack would meet Cody outside the principal's office at three-ten, right after the last bell.

Zack hurried upstairs from his locker to the office. As he rounded the last corner, he saw Kelly standing talking to Cody, and he quickly jumped back before either of them saw him.

"That's okay," he heard Kelly say in a hurt tone. "I just thought that maybe after work, you might want to meet me at the Max."

"Look, Kelly, I told you, I can't," Cody said in a flat tone. "I'm too busy."

"I know. You've been busy a lot lately." Kelly's voice wobbled, and Zack thought she might be close to tears. But then she cleared her throat. "What I mean is, we haven't really had a chance to see each other much this week."

"What's your point, Kelly?" Cody asked stonily.

Now Zack was certain that Kelly was about to cry. "Cody, what's happened?" she asked plaintively. "We were so close. You said all those things last week. . . ."

"That was last week." Cody looked uncomfortable, and he put his hand on the door to the office. "Look, Kelly, I can't talk about it now. Can't you see I'm busy?"

"Yes, I can see that," Kelly said in a subdued voice. "I'm sorry to have bothered you." She turned away and rushed right past Zack without seeing him. It was because her eyes were full of tears.

Zack wanted to race after her and comfort her, but he turned and headed for Cody instead. Cody was still standing, frozen, at the office door. His face was stricken.

"Zack," Cody said. "I've got to tell her, man. She's, like, destroyed."

"She'll be okay," Zack said uneasily. He hated to see Kelly upset. But after Ms. Martinet was dismissed, she'd be happy again. Zack would be the hero of the school, and she'd realize that Zack was the only guy for her. Kelly would probably forgive Cody for hurting her, but it might be hard for her to trust him again. Anyway, she'd be so dazzled by

Zack's success that she'd want him back.

Zack thought that there might be a flaw in his plan, and he felt uneasy for a moment. But he had to continue full steam ahead. Anyway, it would all be over tomorrow.

"Let's get to work," he said gruffly to Cody.

Cody looked at his waterproof watch. "Okay, it's three-fifteen. She'll be in the teacher's lounge checking to see how much coffee the teachers drank today. She'll be back in one and a half minutes. Come on."

Quickly, he led Zack into Ms. Martinet's office. He crossed to the desk and showed Zack the timer on it. "See?" he said. "It's a digital thing. Just press the numbers."

"No sweat," Zack said. He dived under the couch. "Okay," he called out to Cody. "I'm all set."

"Say 'check,'" Cody told him. "Isn't that what double agents say to each other?"

"Check, Cody," Zack answered patiently from under the couch.

Cody lingered. "Shouldn't I have a code name?"

Zack rolled his eyes. "If you want a code name, you can have one."

Cody thought a minute. "How about Dude? I'll be Dude One, and you can be Dude Two."

"Okay, Dude One. Now get moving."

"Check, Dude Two. Over and out."

Zack saw Cody's high-top sneakers move out of the room. In exactly thirty seconds, the door opened, and he saw Ms. Martinet's oxfords. They crossed to the desk and out of sight. There was the creak of a chair, and then the electronic sound of the timer being set. Some papers rustled.

Zack peered at his watch. It seemed to take forever before fifteen minutes went by. The timer gave off an electronic beep. Zack heard the slap of a file folder.

"Good," Ms. Martinet muttered. "One segment, one task. Optimum." The timer beeped as Ms. Martinet set it again.

The door opened, and Cody's high tops entered. "Ms. Martinet? Could you come out here a moment?"

Ms. Martinet's voice softened. "Certainly, Cody."

As soon as Ms. Martinet's oxfords had clomped out of the room, Zack wiggled out from underneath the couch, ran to the timer, erased the number that it was counting off, and punched in a new one. Then he ran back and dived under the couch again.

The door opened. "Certainly, Cody. It's all right. Alphabetizing can be difficult." The shoes clumped toward the desk. A file folder opened.

Two minutes later, the timer beeped.

"What the—" Ms. Martinet said. "Only a third of the way through this task," she muttered. "Terrible."

Zack heard the electronic beep of the timer being

set. He waited. The door opened again.

"I'm sorry, Ms. Martinet, but—"

This time, Ms. Martinet's tone was not as welcoming. "Yes, Cody." The oxfords clomped heavily to the door.

Zack squeezed out, ran to the desk, reset the timer, and squeezed back under the couch again with seconds to spare as Ms. Martinet returned.

"Great salute," she muttered. "But somewhat of a dim bulb, poor dear." The desk chair creaked, the papers rustled. Zack checked his watch.

This time, when the buzzer went off too soon, Ms. Martinet slammed her hand down on the desk. "Eloise, get a grip!" she admonished herself. "Concentrate! That should have been a one-segment task!"

Zack grinned. It wasn't even four-thirty, and they were already getting to her. It might be an uncomfortable afternoon for him, but by five o'clock, Ms. Martinet's nerves would be shot. And when she had her cup of tea to calm her nerves, it wouldn't help. Wait until she tasted those three sugar substitutes.

▲   ▼   ▲

Even though his afternoon underneath Ms. Martinet's couch had been a success—she'd run out early, at four-thirty-eight, an amazing occurrence according to Cody—Zack couldn't help feeling low.

Sure, his plan was working so far. Tomorrow Ms. Martinet would still be feeling shaky. Just a few strong pushes and she'd go over the edge. And when he'd called Mrs. Fingerman to "remind" her that her visit to Bayside High was scheduled for tomorrow, she'd said "Of course" in a confused tone. So the school board visit was all set.

He'd even called Mr. Belding to ask him to show up tomorrow. Unfortunately, Mr. Belding wouldn't come to the phone because a marathon showing of "The Beverly Hill Hoboes" reruns was on, but Mrs. Belding had promised to give him the message.

Even though things were going like clockwork, all Zack could think about were the tears in Kelly's eyes. The look on her face as she'd rushed by him haunted his thoughts all afternoon.

Zack climbed into his car for the ride home, unable to get thoughts of Kelly out of his head. Halfway home, he suddenly made a right turn and went out of his way to drive along the coastline. There was a favorite overlook spot that Kelly loved. When she was upset or just wanted to be alone, she'd often go there to watch the sunset. As the orange ball slipped lower in the sky, lighting the clouds with pink and vermilion, Zack slowed his speed and caught sight of Kelly's blue bicycle propped against a tree.

He pulled over into the empty parking area and turned off the ignition. There was a slight chill in the air, now that the sun was departing, so he reached into the backseat for his sweater. Pulling it on, he stepped from the car and headed across the small lot, his footsteps crunching in the gravel.

The gravel changed to grass as he reached the grove of trees that ringed the lot. The light was fading even more as Zack headed down the path toward the overlook. He passed through the deep emerald shadows of the trees and saw her.

She was sitting on a bench, looking out to sea. The breeze lifted her dark hair off her neck and blew it softly behind her. She was huddled in a baseball jacket, looking as small and defenseless as a twelve-year-old. But then she turned and looked at him, and Zack saw a woman's heart in her eyes. He could see even at a glance how much it was hurting.

He slid onto the bench gingerly. "I thought I'd find you here."

Kelly looked out to sea again. The sun had disappeared, but the horizon was still blazing orange and red, and bursts of flaming color still danced on the ocean. "I just needed to get away," she said. "I feel like such a fool. I thought things were really serious with Cody, and it turns out that he doesn't care about me at all."

Zack swallowed. "You don't know that for sure," he said.

She nodded. "I do," she said softly. "Today really convinced me. What should I do, Zack? I still care about him."

Zack thrust his hands into the pockets of his jeans. "Maybe you should act really cold and distant, too," he suggested. "Give him a taste of his own medicine."

"Maybe I should," Kelly agreed with sudden defiance. "Why should I let him hurt me this way?"

"Now you're talking," Zack said encouragingly. "Be mean!"

Kelly's shoulders slumped. "Who am I kidding, Zack? I can't be mean. I don't know how."

"I know," Zack said softly. "That's what I—like about you so much." That was close. He'd almost said the word *love*.

"The truth is," Kelly brooded, "I'm a sap. I trust somebody right off the bat." She turned to Zack. "That's what I've learned with this experience with Cody, Zack. I can't trust so easily. That's why you and the gang are so important. I've known you forever. I can trust you. I should rely on that and not expect to have it so easily with other people."

"Kelly—"

"That's my resolution, Zack. I'm going to stick to my old friends from now on."

Zack didn't say anything. He just looked at her, his heart full. Kelly's big blue eyes were full of tears, and her mouth looked soft and inviting. The darkness enveloped them, and the air was tangy with salt and autumn chill. It was the perfect, romantic moment. Kelly was achingly vulnerable and open to him. It was time for the big payoff.

Zack patted her on the shoulder. "Don't worry, Kelly," he said lamely. "Things might be better tomorrow."

▲   ▼   ▲

The next day, Zack sneaked into school early with a screwdriver. Cody had given him his key to the main office, and no one had arrived yet when Zack carefully turned the key and pushed open the door. He went directly to Ms. Martinet's office, where he headed for the PA system. In a moment, he had disconnected the wires.

Zack headed for the main office again. Cody had told him that the bells were electronically controlled to ring every fifty minutes. Zack had a pretty good idea how to mess up the schedule.

He hesitantly regarded the timer console. This was definitely more complicated than Ms. Martinet's little digital timer. He crouched over the system, trying to figure it out. How hard could it be? Cody had told him it would be a breeze. But then again, Cody hadn't even figured out how to program his VCR yet.

Zack experimentally pushed a few buttons. It looked like each floor's bells were rigged separately. That meant he could change the codes so that one floor's bells would ring at different times than the others. It would be perfect.

Zack pushed the button that read CHANGE PROGRAM. He read the list of options and pressed the button for the first floor. The first bell was scheduled to ring at 8:20 as a warning, then 8:25 for homeroom. Zack changed the 8:20 warning bell to 8:30, then moved all the other bells back by fifteen minutes. Then he pressed the button for the second-floor bells. It was hard to read in the dimness, but he didn't dare turn on a light.

Just then, every single light in the office blazed to life. "Can I help you, Mr. Morris?" an icy voice demanded.

Chapter 10

Slowly, Zack turned around. Mr. Monza was standing with his hand on the light switch, staring at him.

Zack gave him a dazzling smile. "Hi, there, Mr. Monza. You know, I've been meaning to tell you. I really like your mustache."

Mr. Monza took a few steps into the room. "Don't give me that horse spit, Morris. What are you doing in here?"

"Mrs. Gibbs asked me to, uh, clean up her desk," Zack improvised. He began shifting papers around on Mrs. Gibbs's desk, which was next to where he'd been working.

"Uh-huh," Mr. Monza said. He didn't sound convinced. "Tell me another one."

"And those coveralls!" Zack said nervously.

"What a fashion statement. Where can I get a pair?"

Mr. Monza loomed over him, his hands on his hips. "Spill it, kid."

Zack gave up. He knew Mr. Monza was too sharp to swallow a story. "Look, it's all part of a plan to get rid of Ms. Martinet," he confessed. "Okay, it was stupid of me, I admit it. We all just really want Mr. Belding back." He stuck the screwdriver in his pocket. "I'll just go now."

He tried to walk past Mr. Monza, but the maintenance chief clapped a beefy hand on his arm. Zack was halted in his tracks. His heart hammered against his chest. It was all over. Mr. Monza would turn him in to Ms. Martinet, and he'd never be seen again.

"Get rid of Martinet?" Mr. Monza roared. "Why didn't you say so in the first place? That battle-ax is making my life miserable. Let's get to work."

▲   ▼   ▲

At 8:17 Zack positioned himself by the teachers' mailboxes so that he could see inside Ms. Martinet's office. The bell was silent at 8:20. At 8:21, she began pacing. At 8:22, she came out into the office and demanded to know why the bell hadn't rung. By 8:25, she had sent for Mr. Monza, and when he didn't arrive by 8:29, she was frantic.

Zack ran out of the office and into the hall. He expected students to be milling around, wondering aloud what was wrong. But Ms. Martinet had trained them well. They stood in silence, passively waiting for the bell to ring. When it did, they began to move toward their homerooms.

Zack frowned. The student body was so brainwashed that they couldn't even react normally! And something else was wrong, too, Zack realized. Lisa, Jessie, and Kelly were supposed to have gotten the word out to the rest of the girls to wear miniskirts. Slater was supposed to have talked to the guys about shorts. But everybody was dressed in pants and conservative man-tailored shirts.

As a matter of fact, he was the only one who had dressed crazily today. Zack looked down at himself. He was wearing green jams and a fluorescent orange top. He had spiked his hair straight up. Next to the rest of the students, he looked like an idiot.

Ms. Martinet emerged from the office behind him. She clapped her hands. "That's right, students. Nothing to worry about. Just a little problem with the bells. And the PA system has malfunctioned. I'll be patrolling the halls today to make sure we stay on track. Check the clocks and proceed as usual. And remember the four D's," she called. "Discipline. Diligence. Dedication. Destiny!"

Zack headed for his homeroom, shaking his head. This was going to be harder than he'd thought. Ms. Martinet's influence was running deep. Had she managed to get complete mind control of Bayside High?

▲   ▼   ▲

All that morning, the bells rang erratically. Zack waited hopefully for chaos, but students simply ignored them and followed their usual schedule. Even the gang seemed to be following Ms. Martinet's orders. Maybe they were just waiting until they saw that Ms. Martinet was beginning to crack before they risked their necks to go crazy in the halls. But Zack couldn't wait. Didn't the gang understand that Ms. Martinet would need a major push toward her breakdown? Finally, after the third-period bell, Zack took matters into his own hands. He tried to inject some confusion by racing through the halls, laughing maniacally, but Mr. Dickerson just sent him to the nurse.

Zack left the nurse's office feeling downcast. His plan was flopping—and fast. What he needed was something big, something dramatic. Something Morris-sized.

Zack caught sight of long, glossy dark hair in the hall ahead of him. Kelly! He rushed forward, then stopped and watched her. Kelly was walking in a stiff fashion that was totally unlike her usual graceful moves. He noticed that she was wearing khaki pants and a crisply pressed khaki shirt. The outfit was kind of dull for Kelly. She liked soft colors and pretty fabrics.

Zack caught up to her as she reached her locker. "Kelly, it's all up to us," he said.

She turned. "Us?"

Zack nodded. "The plan. We have to shift into high gear. I think a food fight is in order. We can start it at lunch. The special is tuna casserole. It'll be perfect."

A fine line appeared between Kelly's eyebrows. "A food fight? That would be so . . . messy."

"Right," Zack said encouragingly. "That's the point."

Kelly's frown deepened. "So . . . disorganized."

"Exactly," Zack went on. "Listen, I'm glad I saw you alone. I wanted to see how you were. You were pretty upset last night, and I—"

"The situation has stabilized," Kelly said in an uncharacteristic monotone.

Stabilized? Zack stared at her in disbelief. Something was different, all right. Kelly's blue eyes were blank instead of sparkling. Her full mouth was pressed in a thin line. Her normally welcoming expression was forbidding. "Kelly?" Zack said. "Are you okay?"

"Situation normal," Kelly said. She sounded like a computer.

"Kelly," Zack said urgently, "what's the matter? This isn't like you."

She turned her blank gaze on him. "I don't know what you mean, Zack. I'm fine."

"Kelly, I said you should be cold to *Cody*. Not to me. I'm your oldest—and best—friend, remember? Remember what you said last night?"

Kelly took a book out of her locker and slammed it shut. "I have to go, Zack. I have a fifteen-minute segment to accomplish a twenty-minute task."

Zack stumbled backward. Kelly had turned into a Ms. Martinet clone! She moved away, and he touched her arm. "Wait," he said desperately. "You can't turn off your emotions like this. Kelly, Cody isn't worth it. Don't be upset."

Kelly's expression was dead. "Cody?" she asked in an expressionless tone. "I'm not upset about him at all. It doesn't matter anymore. Love is so messy, anyway." Then she marched away.

▲   ▼   ▲

Reeling, Zack disobeyed the new rules and left the school building. He stumbled outside and walked to the football field. There, he sat down in the deserted bleachers and stared bleakly at the field. He thought of Kelly's empty eyes, and he knew that he had driven her to that emptiness. He had broken her heart as surely as if he had deliberately set out to do exactly that. He had turned her into a coldhearted machine because sweet, gentle Kelly couldn't bear how much she'd been hurt.

Just a few days ago, Kelly's trusting heart had been one of the best things in his life. He could always count on her to give people the benefit of the doubt, to see the best in every situation. Then he'd gone ahead and completely destroyed her trust in all mankind. Kelly might never recover, Zack realized. She had a major scar on her heart that might never heal. And Zack might have lost her forever.

Zack sat, his chin in his hands, and did some hard thinking. He'd been running around so frantically trying to get Kelly back that he hadn't thought about *her* at all. Sure, he loved her with all his heart. But how good could that love be if he could stand by and watch her be hurt?

He must have known, Zack realized. He must have realized, somewhere inside himself, that he'd been a complete pig. Why else hadn't he seized the moment the night before and kissed her?

Because he had felt too guilty. Because he'd known for days that he was doing something wrong.

Zack stood up as the realization rushed through

him. He truly did love Kelly. He knew that for sure now. Now he knew that he only wanted her to be happy, even if being happy meant that she'd be with another guy.

Zack started back toward school, his hands in his pockets, his face set with determination. Loving Kelly the best way he could, he realized, meant he had to let her go.

▲   ▼   ▲

When Zack came back into school, for the first time, he truly saw how changed Bayside High had become. The school was like a prison. Everyone looked gray faced and drab. There was no laughter, no excited chatter in the halls. Had he been so involved in his own problems that he hadn't noticed how terrible the change was?

Zack hurried through the halls. As soon as he told Kelly the truth about Cody, he could return his attention to getting Mr. Belding back again. The bell rang, but nobody left their classrooms. They were waiting for the real time to change classes. All of Mr. Monza's sneaky work had been in vain.

Zack turned a corner and saw Ms. Martinet patrolling with her bat. Quickly, he doubled back and ran the other way. Just ahead, he saw Jessie leave the girls' room and start down the hall.

"Jessie!" he called, hurrying toward her. "Have you seen Kelly?"

Jessie turned. "No," she answered shortly.

"It's really important," Zack said.

"It's time for class," Jessie said mechanically. "You can't have discipline without punctuality."

Zack frowned. "Jessie, is something the matter?"

"Negative." Jessie looked at her watch. "Two minutes to class change."

Baffled, Zack watched Jessie turn away. He stood in the hall as she moved briskly toward the door of her class. The door opened and shut. She was gone. Maybe she was upset about yesterday, when he cut her off at the Max to tell everyone about his plan. He'd have to apologize about that when he had some time.

Zack hurried toward the staircase. Kelly had history third period. He could catch her as she left the classroom, if he was lucky.

But just before he reached her classroom, all the doors in the hall opened at the same exact moment. Students spilled out silently in the hall, walking briskly. Zack saw Lisa ahead of him, dressed in a camouflage outfit.

"Lisa, wait up!" he called, hurrying after her. "Everyone is so weird today," he told her as he swung into step beside her. She was walking so briskly he could hardly keep up.

"No talking in the halls," Lisa advised flatly.

"Lisa, wait up. Where are you headed?"

"Special assembly," Lisa answered in the same flat tone. "Didn't you hear the announcement? The PA system is broken, but a messenger came to every class. Very efficient."

Zack peered into her face. Slowly, the shock registered. "Lisa!" he cried in alarm. "Oh, no!"

"Calm down, Zack," Lisa said tersely. "Remember the first *D*. Discipline."

"But you're not wearing makeup!" Zack exclaimed, horrified.

"Time management is too crucial in the morning," Lisa reported woodenly. "By the way, have you heard about the sale at the army-navy store?"

Zack felt as though he had landed smack into his worst nightmare. What was the matter with everybody? "Lisa, stop acting like a pod person. This is no joke. I really have to find Kelly. Have you seen her?"

Lisa's vacant eyes gazed past him. "Time for assembly," she answered.

Zack stumbled backward as Lisa moved off in a brisk goose step. He needed a dose of reality, and he needed it quick. Someone familiar, someone normal.

"Screech!" he cried. His friend was rounding the corner. Dressed in a plaid shirt, plaid shorts, and combat boots, Screech looked like his usual zany self. *Thank goodness*, Zack thought with relief.

Screech could always be counted on to be completely out of his mind.

Screech came within a foot of Zack. He clicked his heels together and saluted.

"Screech?" Zack said doubtfully.

"Correction," Screech announced in a clipped tone, holding the salute. "That's Major Plaid to you, soldier!"

Chapter 11

Eyes front, Jessie marched toward the auditorium for the special assembly. She wheeled around the corner smartly and ran smack into Slater.

Jessie backed up, confused. "E-excuse me," she stammered. She tried to move past him, but Slater's muscular arm shot out and his hand landed flat against the wall, pinning her in the corner. "It looks like you're outflanked," he said, his eyes gleaming.

Jessie met his gaze uneasily. Her heartbeat fluttered, but she reminded herself that she had a mission. She couldn't let Slater interfere with that. He was always interfering with something—her peace of mind, her control, her pulse. She might jeer at his macho attitude, but something about the guy stirred her up.

But that didn't mean she had to let him know it. "Assembly is at eleven hundred hours," she said crisply. "It's time to move out."

"Affirmative," Slater shot back. "But first, I think some personal negotiations are in order."

"Personal negotiations?" Jessie's chin lifted. "Explain."

Slater withdrew his arm and put his hands in his pockets. "Our skirmishes are counterproductive," he rapped out. "When two hostile enemy forces dig in for a siege, sometimes the best strategy is a new attempt at peace talks."

"I see," Jessie said slowly. "What do you propose?"

"Instead of scaling the fortifications," Slater said, "I'd like the walls to come tumbling down. In other words—" He hesitated.

"In other words?"

He grinned. "Lay down your arms. It's time for a truce."

Jessie tossed her head. "What if I dig in instead?" she asked.

Slater moved closer. "I counterattack. And I have very deadly weapons."

There was a glint in Slater's eyes that sent her heartbeat racing even faster. Jessie stepped back and hit the wall again. "I'm a pacifist, remember?" she asked uneasily.

"Mmmm, I remember," Slater said, taking another step toward her. He slipped his arms around her. "And I'm counting on it."

"Hey," Jessie protested. Her voice came out a little breathless. "What do you call this?"

Slater grinned. "Elementary military strategy, compadre." He squeezed her gently. "A pincer movement."

"A sneak attack?" Jessie's lips curved in a reluctant smile.

"Not at all," Slater responded softly. "It's just smart diplomacy." He bent his head and his lips brushed hers. He kissed her softly and surely. Jessie's head fell back, and the world dropped away as she kissed him back. Her senses whirled and her fingertips tingled as she ran her hands up his arms and entwined them around his neck.

Finally, they drew apart slowly. Jessie gulped. "They could really use you in the UN," she told Slater dazedly.

▲   ▼   ▲

Zack charged to the phone outside the cafeteria, lifted the receiver, and quickly punched out Mr. Belding's number. The assembly was due to start in seven minutes, and he had a feeling that with Ms. Martinet in charge, it wouldn't be one second later.

He counted off the rings, praying that Mr. Belding would answer.

"Hello?"

Zack closed his eyes in relief. It was Mr. Belding. "It's Zack, Mr. Belding," he said quickly. "I don't have time to talk. But you have to get to Bayside High right away."

"But I'm watching 'Whirl of Fortune.'"

"Mr. Belding," Zack cried in frustration, "I know being out of work has been rough on you. But what happened to all your talk about responsibility to Bayside High? Did that go away just because you're not here anymore?"

The phone line hummed with silence.

"Please, Mr. Belding," Zack pleaded. "Ms. Martinet is ruining the school. We need you."

There was a long silence. "I'm sorry, Zack," Mr. Belding finally said in a sad voice. "I just can't." Then Zack heard a soft click.

He rested his head against the phone for a minute. He couldn't believe that Mr. Belding had let him down. But who was he to talk? He'd let down the whole school, too. Not to mention Kelly.

Kelly! Zack raced toward the auditorium. Students were standing in rows outside, facing forward, waiting for the doors to open. Zack ran through the crowd frantically. There was no sign of Kelly anywhere.

Zack passed Kelly three times before he realized

it was her. She was just another khaki-clad student leaning against a wall, staring blankly at the auditorium doors. He had been looking for flash and sparkle, not a zombie. He had been looking for Kelly, and he'd forgotten that the Kelly he loved and adored had been taken over by a Ms. Martinet clone.

He touched her arm, and she turned to him. "Oh, hi, Zack," she said in a remote voice. "The assembly should only take one-and-a-half fifteen-minute time segments."

"Kelly, please come with me," Zack begged. "I have to tell you something. It's important."

He didn't give her a chance to protest but took her by the arm, pulled her into an empty classroom, and closed the door.

"This is highly irregular," Kelly said tonelessly. "We were instructed to wait outside the auditorium."

"Kelly, I have to tell you about Cody," Zack said firmly. "There's something you don't know."

Kelly turned away, and he couldn't see her face. "I've been completely debriefed."

"No, you haven't. Kelly, Cody has been working under cover. I asked him to become Ms. Martinet's assistant and spy on her. And to do that, he had to gain her confidence. He had to break up with you. I swore him to secrecy. Look, it's all my fault. I'm sorry, Kelly."

Kelly kept her face turned away. Her fingers picked at the wood of an empty desk.

Zack's throat was tight. It was the hardest thing in the world to do, but he had to do it. "Cody really cares about you," he said. "He never stopped. He'd explain it all to you if you'd let him."

The door burst open, and Ms. Martinet stood in the doorway, her hands on her hips. "What are you two doing in here?" she demanded.

Kelly snapped to attention. "Sorry, Ms. Martinet."

"Time for assembly," Ms. Martinet reminded them, her gray eyes icy.

"Yes, ma'am," Kelly said. She whirled around and marched toward the door.

Zack started after her. "Kelly—"

"Assembly," Kelly interrupted flatly. "No talking."

Zack stood still, watching Kelly march away. He didn't understand it. Kelly hadn't reacted to his news at all. She was still an automaton. She was completely under Ms. Martinet's control!

▲   ▼   ▲

A shrill whistle blew as Zack slipped in a side door of the auditorium and melted into the shadows. He wasn't about to take his place in line and perform like a robot for Ms. Martinet. He could see the school board lined up in front of the auditorium, waiting for the students to file in. It was Ms. Martinet's show, Zack thought bitterly. She would demonstrate how efficiently she'd taken control, and the board would probably extend her contract for another fifty years. His plan had failed completely.

Another whistle split the air, and the back doors opened. Ms. Martinet appeared. She blew her whistle again. "Ten-*hut!*" she shouted.

The students marched in, with Jessie standing tall at their head. They moved in perfect formation to the front of the auditorium, their footsteps thundering in time. Zack saw Lisa, Kelly, and Screech at the head of the column. Even easygoing Slater had joined in. He was at the front of the entire football and wrestling teams. They were all wearing T-shirts that read FUTURE MEMBERS OF ROTC.

Jessie blew her own whistle, and the students marched into their rows. They stood at attention, waiting. Jessie blew her whistle again, and they sat simultaneously, faces front. Jessie whirled around and clicked her heels while Ms. Martinet watched in approval. Cody Durant was at her side, standing at attention.

"All present and accounted for, ma'am," Jessie announced.

Zack saw the school board members turn to each other and murmur. Ms. Martinet beamed.

Mrs. Fingerman stepped forward. "First of all, we'd like to apologize for disrupting your school day," she said with a smile.

Jessie snapped to attention. "We are trained to react to the unexpected, ma'am."

Mrs. Fingerman nodded. "Admirable." She turned to Ms. Martinet. "The school seems to have undergone a change from the last time we visited. And you've had such a short time here, Ms. Martinet."

Ms. Martinet smiled modestly. "They were crying out for discipline, Mrs. Fingerman."

"Well," Mrs. Fingerman said to the auditorium, "I hope you're all ready for the big game against Central High this weekend."

Slater stood and shook his head. "Negative, Mrs. Fingerman. The football team has disbanded."

Next to him, Kelly stood. "Cheerleaders, too. Discipline and work are more important," she said. "No time for trivial pursuits."

Slater and Kelly sat down again. "I see," Mrs. Fingerman said. She looked at Ms. Martinet.

"The grade-point averages of Bayside High have already shown great improvement," Ms. Martinet told her proudly.

"That's very, uh, good." Mrs. Fingerman stepped back and began to confer with the rest of the board. Zack watched them put their heads together and murmur, shooting occasional glances at

Ms. Martinet and Jessie, who was still standing at attention. There was not a murmur, a cough, or a foot shuffle from the rest of the auditorium. The perfect school sat in perfect silence.

Zack felt as though his whole life was going down the drain. He gazed around hopelessly. Mr. Belding hadn't shown up. There was nobody to counteract Ms. Martinet. Nobody to speak out about how she'd changed the school for the worse.

Nobody except him.

Zack bolted from the back of the auditorium. "Excuse me!" he yelled as he quickly hurried down the aisle. "Mrs. Fingerman? I have something to say to the board!"

"Mr. Morris!" Ms. Martinet bellowed. "Get back into your seat right now!"

"I'm sorry, Ms. Martinet," Zack said. "I have to say something first."

"Students have no voice here. Mr. Morris, get into your seat." Now Ms. Martinet hissed through her teeth. "Immediately."

Zack stopped in front of the board. Jessie shot him a warning look, but he ignored it. She might be a Ms. Martinet clone, but he still had his own mind.

"Mr. Morris, you are facing suspension," Ms. Martinet warned icily.

"I don't care. I—"

"You are suspended, Mr. Morris."

"I don't care," Zack said, his chin high. He spoke directly to the board. "Last week, I was principal for only a day," he said. "And it only took me one day to see how important a principal is, because I really messed up. What happened last Wednesday was all my fault. It wasn't Mr. Belding's. I misused my power as principal and everything got all mixed up. That's how I know how dangerous the misuse of power can be." He gave Ms. Martinet a meaningful look, and her eyes widened.

Zack held out an arm and swept the auditorium. "You may not see it, but everyone else in this auditorium has learned the same lesson. Everyone is scared to death of Ms. Martinet. Mr. Belding was our principal, but he was always our friend, too. He talked about freedom and discipline going hand in hand. Now we know exactly what he means. And everyone here misses him. Even *I* miss him. We want him back, Mrs. Fingerman. He was fired because of my mistake. That's what was great about Mr. Belding—he let us make mistakes. He said that sometimes that was the best way to learn."

Zack turned around to leave. He looked up the aisle to the back of the auditorium and saw Mr. Belding standing against the door. He had even changed out of his bathrobe. Zack grinned.

Ms. Martinet spoke up next to him. Her face was rigid with anger. "Well, you've just made a big mistake, Morris. You've disrupted this school once too often. Mr. Belding might encourage you, but I won't. Go and clean out your locker. You are hereby expelled!"

Chapter 12

At first, there was only shocked silence in the auditorium. Then Kelly stood up. "No!" she shouted.

"Miss Kapowski, sit down!" Ms. Martinet roared.

Zack saw Mr. Belding push off the back wall and take a faltering step toward the front. "Mrs. Fingerman," he started. His voice cracked, and he cleared his throat as every head in the auditorium turned to look at him. "Mrs. Fingerman," he said again, his voice stronger now, "I must object. Surely expulsion is too harsh a punishment for outspokenness. If I had expelled Zack Morris for speaking out, he wouldn't have made it past freshman year."

"Hah!" Ms. Martinet snorted. "That's just the

problem, Mr. Belding. It's students like Morris that bring down the whole school."

"It's students like Morris that give Bayside High its imagination and its spirit," Mr. Belding answered softly. He winked at Zack. "He's worth the trouble most of the time."

"Thanks, Mr. Belding," Zack said.

"I didn't say *all* of the time," Mr. Belding warned.

Ms. Martinet blew her whistle, and they all covered their ears. "This is inexcusable!" she exclaimed angrily. "You are no longer the principal of Bayside High, Mr. Belding!"

"Excuse me," Mrs. Fingerman broke in smoothly as the two principals glared at each other. "Mr. Belding, I'm afraid Ms. Martinet is right. You are no longer the principal of Bayside High. Policy decisions are not yours to make."

Ms. Martinet shot Mr. Belding a triumphant look. "Martinet's Rules of Order win again," she said. "The four *D*'s always guarantee success."

"Excuse me, Ms. Martinet," Mrs. Fingerman said. "But you are no longer the principal of Bayside High, either. You have been removed by the unanimous vote of the board."

"W-what?" Ms. Martinet sputtered.

Mrs. Fingerman looked at her disapprovingly. "We are shocked at what Bayside High has turned into—an army camp, not a school! What have you done to these students, Ms. Martinet? I see no spark of liveliness here, no curiosity, no joy. This used to be a school of energy and laughter as well as hard work."

"Laughter?" Ms. Martinet asked, baffled.

Mrs. Fingerman turned to Mr. Belding. "And maybe it can be again. If Mr. Belding will return."

The auditorium erupted into wild applause. Cheers rocked the hall, and every student stood and screamed for Mr. Belding's return. Finally, Mrs. Fingerman held up a hand for quiet. "What do you say, Mr. Belding?"

Mr. Belding grinned. "I guess I have no choice. I accept!"

The auditorium exploded with more applause. The entire board laughed as Zack, Slater, Jessie, Lisa, and Screech all surrounded Mr. Belding and clapped him on the back so hard he almost slid the rest of the way down the aisle. Ms. Martinet, her mouth tight, marched up the aisle and disappeared out the door.

"By the way," Mrs. Fingerman shouted above the din, "what *are* the four D's, anyway?"

Cody leaped to the front of the auditorium and held up a hand. "I have them," he announced, and paused. "Defiant dudes dodge dictator!" he yelled, and a roar went up from the students. Everyone stomped their feet and whistled.

Zack couldn't believe it. Maybe Cody did have

half a brain, after all. Then Zack saw Kelly run down the aisle toward Cody. He opened his arms, and she flew into them. Zack turned away.

Funny, he thought, confused. Now Kelly was totally back to normal. But why had she acted like a zombie in the first place? And why had Jessie, Slater, Lisa, and Screech all acted so weird? They had totally gone along with Ms. Martinet during the assembly. Why hadn't they spoken up to the board?

Jessie saw the confusion on his face and walked over. "What's the matter, Zack?" she asked. "You look a little mystified."

"What happened to all of you, Jessie?" Zack asked. "Ms. Martinet really got to you. How could you have fallen for her mind control, anyway? You guys really scared me."

Jessie grinned. Her hazel eyes sparkled with mischief, and she poked Zack rather hard. "That will teach you not to listen to me, you dweeb," she said. "It was all part of my plan."

"*Your* plan?" Zack asked.

"You're not the only one with a scheming brain, Zack Morris," Jessie told him crisply. "I realized that the best way to get rid of Ms. Martinet was simply to *obey* her. Turn into perfect soldier clones. If you carry Ms. Martinet's philosophy to its extreme, you get an army camp, just like Mrs. Fingerman said. I knew that the board would freak out if they saw that. Much better than if we all went crazy and were worse than ever. So I got everyone to go along."

Zack felt hurt. "You could have told me, Jessie," he said. "I was really worried about everyone. Especially Kelly."

Jessie gave him a sharp look. "Kelly's just fine. And if you hadn't been so rude, you would have been in on it. We all know you're good at talking. It's time you got good at listening, too."

"You're right, Jessie," Zack admitted. "I should have listened to you. I've been crazed all week. I'm sorry."

Jessie patted him gently. "Well, you've learned a lesson, anyway."

"I sure have," Zack said fervently. "I'll never shut you up again."

Slater appeared behind Jessie. "That's right, preppie. That's *my* job."

Jessie twisted around and tried to swat him playfully. But instead, Slater leaned over and kissed her nose. They looked at each other and smiled into each other's eyes.

"It looks like you two have made up," Zack said with a smile. He was happy for Slater and Jessie, but he couldn't help feeling sad, too. He looked over their heads at Kelly and Cody, and he felt a sharp pang. Cody had his arms around Kelly, and he was talking to her softly. She was gazing up at him as though he were the greatest thing she'd ever seen.

Zack sighed. He felt like a failure. Everything he'd planned had completely backfired. Mr. Belding had been rehired, sure. But the most important part of his plan had fallen through. Kelly was more in love with Cody than ever.

Just then, Kelly looked over and saw Zack watching her. She waved, and smiled, then walked toward him, arm in arm with Cody. "Thank you, Zack," she said when she reached him. "I'm glad you told me about Cody before assembly. If you hadn't, I don't know if I would have listened to him when he tried to explain. I probably would have told him to jump off a cliff," she said, giggling. "Instead, I just went to him and told him that I knew." She leaned over and kissed Zack's cheek. "It was really thoughtful."

The kiss was totally passionless, the kiss of a good friend. Zack swallowed. "Anytime, Kelly."

"Thanks from me, too, man," Cody said. "I've finally been accepted by the kids at Bayside High, thanks to you. Not to mention," he said, smiling at Kelly, "that thanks to you, I have Kelly again."

"No problem," Zack said. "I'm glad I could help." He watched them walk away, hand in hand. Kelly's head brushed against Cody's shoulder and his arm went around her. Zack's heart felt like it had been banged repeatedly with a hammer.

"Zack?" Jessie appeared at his side. She followed his gaze to Kelly and Cody, and looked back at him sharply. "You still love Kelly, don't you?" she guessed shrewdly.

Zack didn't bother lying to his best friend. Jessie knew him too well. He nodded. "I just realized it this week," he confessed. "My feelings for her never went away. I don't think they ever will."

Jessie slipped her arm through his. "I think you did the right thing, Zack," she told him firmly. "Kelly needs to find out how she really feels about Cody. If she doesn't, she'll always wonder about him. Giving her up was the smartest move you ever made."

"Oh, really?" Zack asked. "Then why do I feel so dumb?"

Jessie's hazel eyes were full of compassion, and she hugged him gently and moved away. Slater came up to her, and the two of them walked up the aisle hand in hand. Kelly and Cody joined them, their arms around each other. Then the foursome headed for the exit.

Suddenly, Mr. Belding appeared at Zack's elbow. "By the way," Mr. Belding said, "I haven't told you what my first policy decision is as your newly reinstated principal."

"What's that, Mr. Belding?" Zack asked. He wasn't very interested, but Mr. Belding looked pretty cheerful.

"To reinstate *you*," Mr. Belding told him. "You were expelled, remember?"

"Oh, right." Zack sighed. He didn't really care anymore if he was expelled or not. As a matter of fact, it would be better if he was. How could he come to school every day and see Kelly and Cody together?

The auditorium door shut with a *whoosh*. Silence echoed in the empty hall. Together, Zack and Mr. Belding silently headed up the aisle.

Mr. Belding slung an arm around Zack's shoulder. "You know, Zack, I think this is the beginning of a beautiful friendship."

Zack felt like a character in an old black-and-white movie. A fantasy floated into his mind. He was standing on a fog-shrouded runway. He had a trench coat, a hat, and a lisp. His gaze was tragic as he stood and watched the woman he loved walk off with another man. He felt very noble and very sad.

But wait—this was *his* fantasy. His movie. Zack could rewrite the ending any way he wanted!

A grin slowly spread over Zack's face. Maybe this was only part one of the story. With a little scheming, a little scamming, the tide could turn. Kelly just might turn out to be his heroine after all.